Robert Williams Buchanan

White Rose and Red

A love Story

Robert Williams Buchanan

White Rose and Red
A love Story

ISBN/EAN: 9783337076863

Printed in Europe, USA, Canada, Australia, Japan

Cover: Foto ©Andreas Hilbeck / pixelio.de

More available books at **www.hansebooks.com**

THE RED FLAG

And other Poems.

BY THE HON. RODEN NOEL,

AUTHOR OF "BEATRICE AND OTHER POEMS."

Small 8vo, 6s.

" There are poetry and power of a high order in the volume before us. The
'Red Flag' is a terrible and thunderous poem. There are fine sympathies
with the sorrows of London life and wonderful knowledge of them. Perhaps
one of the most solemn, awful poems of the present century is ' The Vision of
the Desert.' . . . Let his imagination and metaphysical faculty be well yoked
and guided by his own cultivated taste, and we must all admit the advent of a
great poet."—*British Quarterly Review.*

" Mr. Noel's new volume marks a decided advance both in clearness of form
and in melody of expression upon his earlier collection. He has succeeded in
working out more unity of style, in harmonizing his thought and feeling, and
in producing more sustained effects of music in verse without sacrificing indi-
viduality. . . . It is probably upon the compositions of the third and fourth
sections that the reputation of Mr. Noel as a poet of marked originality will
ultimately rest. The situation of ' The Red Flag' is finely conceived and
powerfully presented. The sincerity of the poet, his intense feeling for the
terrible, the realism with which he has wrought every detail of his picture,
and his passionate sympathy with the oppressed, make the general effect of this
poem very impressive. In ' Palingenesis' and ' Richmond Hill' and the ' Sea
Symphony' Mr. Noel exhibits a rarer quality of artistic production. These
poems are steeped in thought and feeling: Nature is represented with the
most minute and patient accuracy, yet each description is pervaded with a
sense of that divine mysterious life that throbs within the world. We need to
travel back to the Bhagavadgita or to take Walt Whitman from the shelf if we
seek to match the pantheistic enthusiasm of the climax to ' Palingenesis.'
The promise of Mr. Noel's earlier poem in this style, ' Pan,' is here fulfilled."
—*Academy.*

" There is much unpalatable truth in this satire, sometimes very cleverly
put. . . . . We do not think any lover of poetry can read ' The Water-Nymph
and the Boy,' ' Allerheiligen,' or ' Palingenesis,' without enjoying and
admiring the exquisitely coloured word-pictures they contain."—*Scotsman.*

" A volume of very remarkable poems. There are a richness of thought,
a power of language, a wild, rushing, cataract-like movement of melody,
and an originality of purpose almost unique among the rising poets of the
age, in this volume. It will be Mr. Noel's own fault if he does not take the
very highest rank among his contemporary poets."—*Dundee Advertiser.*

" A singular book, in which there is much real poetic force and feeling."—
Graphic.

" Our skeleton sketch gives little notion of the earnest power of this noble
poem. . . . The volume will reach and please a wider circle than the last, and
we believe that future volumes will soon make the writer's name familiar to
all appreciative readers of good English poetry."—*Weekly Review.*

" The lines we have italicised seem to us to be worthy of the very foremost
of our living poets."—*Freeman.*

" The writer has more than that love of nature which spends itself on the
beauty of form and colour; he is alive to that more spiritual emotion which
connects the aspects of outward nature with the aspirations of the human soul.
. . . In spite of these faults, he is capable on occasions of writing noble
passages."—*Spectator.*

" In striking contrast to the tone and manner and rhythm of the opening
poem is the succeeding one, entitled ' April Gleams.' It is dainty as gossamer,
fanciful, dreamy, suggestive of summer melodies and woodland brooks."—
Morning Post.

STRAHAN & CO., 56, LUDGATE HILL, LONDON.

WHITE ROSE AND RED

WHITE ROSE AND RED

A Love Story

BY THE AUTHOR OF "ST. ABE"

STRAHAN & CO.
56, LUDGATE HILL, LONDON
1873

LONDON:
PRINTED BY VIRTUE AND CO
CITY ROAD.

CONTENTS.

———◆———

viii

CONTENTS.

PART IV.—THE GREAT SNOW.

INVOCATION.

·

" KNOW'ST THOU THE LAND?"

I.

Know'st thou the Land, where the lian-flower
Burgeons the trapper's forest bower,
Where o'er his head the acacia sweet
Shaketh her scented locks in the heat,
Where the hang-bird swings to a blossom-cloud,
And the bobolink sings merry and loud?
Know'st thou the Land?

     O there! O there,
Might I with thee, O friend of my heart, repair!

II.

Know'st thou the Land where the golden Day
Flowers into glory and glows away,
While the Night springs up, as an Indian girl
Clad in purple and hung with pearl!

INVOCATION.

.And the white **Moon's** heaven rolls **apart,**
Like a bell-shaped flower with **a golden heart,—**
Know'st **thou** the Land?

               O there ! O there,
Might I with thee, O Maid of my Soul, repair !

III.

Know'st thou the Land where the woods are free,
And the prairie rolls as a mighty sea,
And over its waves the sunbeams shine,
While on its misty horizon-line
Dark and dim the buffaloes stand,
And the hunter is gliding gun in hand?
Know'st thou it well?

              O there! O there,
Might I, with those whose Souls are free, repair

IV.

Know'st thou the **Land** where the sun-bird's song
Filleth the forest **all** day long,
Where all is music and mirth and bloom,
Where the cedar sprinkles a soft **perfume,**

Where life is gay as a glancing **stream,**
And all things answer the Poet's dream?
Know'st thou the Land?

                O there! O there,
Might I, with him who loves my lays, repair!

V.

Know'st thou the Land where the **swampy brakes**
Are full of the nests of the rattlesnakes,
Where round old Grizzly the wild **bees hum,**
While squatting he sucks at their honeycomb,
Where crocodiles crouch and the wild cat springs,
And the mildest ills are mosquito stings?
Know'st thou the Land?

                O there! O there,
Might I, with adverse Critics, straight repair!

VI.

Know'st thou the Land where **wind and sun**
Smile on all races of men—save one:
Where (strange and wild as a sunset proud
Streak'd with the bars of a thunder-cloud)

Alone **and** *silent the Red Man lies,*

Sees **the** *cold stars coming, and sinks,* **and dies?**

Know'st thou the Land?

> *O there! O there,*

Might I to *wet his poor parch'd lips repair!*

VII.

Lock up *thy gold, and take thy flight*

To the *mighty Land of the red* **and white;**

A *ditty of love I would have thee hear,*

While *daylight dies, and the Night comes near*

With her black feet wet from the western sea,

And the *Red Man dies, with* **his eyes on** *thee!*

Fast to that Land, ere his *last footprints there*

Are beaten down by alien feet, repair!

Part I.

THE CAPTURE OF EUREKA HART.

B

NATURA NATURANS.

Dawn breaking. Thro' his dew-veil smiles the
    sun,
  And under him doth run
On the green grass and in the forest brake
  Bright beast and speckled snake;
Birds on the bough and insects in the ray
  Gladden; and it is day.

What is this lying on the thymy steep,
  Where yellow bees hum deep,
And the rich air is warm as living breath?
  What soft shape slumbereth
Naked and dark, and glows in a green nest,
  Low-breathing in bright rest?

Is it the spotted panther, lying there
　Lissome and light and fair?
Is it the snake, with glittering skin coil'd round
　And gleaming on the ground?
Is it some wondrous bird whose eyrie lies
　Between the earth and skies?
'Tis none of these, but something stranger far—
　Strange as a fallen star!
A mortal birth, a marvel heavenly-eyed,
　With dark pink breast and side!
And as she lies the wild deer comes most meek
　To smell her scented cheek,
And creeps away; the yeanling ounce lies near,
　And watches with no fear;
The serpent rustles past, with touch as light
　As rose-leaves, rippling bright
Into the grass beyond; while yonder, on high,
　A black speck in the sky,
The crested eagle hovers, with sharp sight
　Facing the flood of light.

What living shape is this who sleeping lies
   Watch'd by all wondering eyes
Of beast and speckled snake and flying bird?
   Softly she sleeps, unstirr'd
By wind or sun; and since she first fell there
   Her raven locks of hair
Have loosen'd, shaken round her in a shower,
   Whence, like a poppy flower
With dark leaves and a tongue to brightness
    tipt,
   She lies vermillion-lipt.
Bare to the waist, her head upon her arm,
   Coil'd on a couch most warm
Of balsam and of hemlock, whose soft scent
   With her warm breath is blent.
Around her brow a circlet of pure gold,
   With antique letters scroll'd,
Burns in the sun-ray, and with gold also
   Her wrists and ancles glow.
Around her neck the threaded wild cat's teeth

Hang white as pearl; beneath
Her bosoms heave, and in the space between,
  Duskly tattoo'd, is seen
A figure small as of a pine-bark brand
  Held blazing in a hand.
Her skirt of azure, wrought with braid and thread
  In quaint signs yellow and red,
Scarce reaches to her dark and dimpled knee,
  Leaving it bare and free.
Below, mocassins red as blood are wound,
  With gold and purple bound ;—
So that red-footed like the stork she lies,
  With softly shrouded eyes,
Whose brightness seems with heavy lustrous
    dew
  To pierce the dark lids thro'.
Her eyelids closed, her poppied lips apart,
  And her quick eager heart
Stirring her warm frame, as a bird unseen
  Stirs the warm lilac-sheen,

She slumbers,—and of all beneath the skies
  Seemeth the last to rise.

She stirs—she wakens—now, O birds, sing loud
  Under the golden cloud!
She stirs — she wakens — now, O wild beast,
    spring,
  Blooms grow, breeze blow, birds sing!
She wakens in her nest and looks around,
  And listens to the sound;
Her eyelids blink against the heavens' bright
    beam,
  Still dim and dark with dream,
Her breathing quickens, and her cheek gleams
    red,
  And round her shining head
Glossy her black hair glistens. Now she stands,
  And with her little hands
Shades her soft orbs and upward at the sky
  She gazeth quietly;

Then at one bound springs with a sudden song
  The forest-track along.

Thro' the transparent roof of twining leaves,
  Where the deep sunlight weaves
Threads like a spider's-web of silvern white,
  Faint falls the dreamy light
Down the gray bolls and boughs that intervene,
  On to the carpet green
Prinkt with all wondrous flowers, on emerald
    brakes
  Where the still speckled snakes
Crawl shaded; and above the shaded ground,
  Amid the deep-sea sound
Of the high branches, bright birds scream and fly
  And chattering parrots cry;
And everywhere beneath them in the bowers
  Float things like living flowers,
Hovering and settling; and here and there
  The blue gleams deep and fair

Thro' the high **parted** boughs, while serpent-
bright
Slips thro' **the** golden light,
Startling the cool deep shades that brood around,
And floating to the ground,
With multitudinous living motes **at play**
Like dust in the rich ray.

Hither for shelter from the burning sun
Hath stolen the beauteous one,
And thro' the ferns and flowers she runs, and
plucks   .
Berries blue-black, and sucks
The fallen orange.   Where the sunbeams blink
She lieth down to drink
Out of the deep pool, and her image sweet
Floats dim below her feet,
Up-peering thro' the lilies yellow and white
And green leaves where the bright

Great Dragon-fly doth pause.   With burning
   breath
   She looks and gladdeneth.
She holds her hands, the shape holds out hands too;
   She stoops more near to view,
And it too stoopeth looking wild and sly;
   Whereat, with merry cry,
She starteth up, and fluttering onward flies
   With gladness in her eyes.

But who is this who all alone lies deep
   In heavy-lidded sleep?
A dark smile hovering on his bearded lips,
   His hunter's gun he grips,
And snores aloud where snakes and lizards run,
   His mighty limbs i' the sun
And his fair face within the shadow.   See!
   His breath comes heavily
Like one's tired out with toil; and when in fear
   The Indian maid comes near,

And bendeth over him most wondering,
　The bright birds scream and sing,
The motes are madder in the ray, the snake
　Glides luminous in the brake,
The sunlight flashes fiery overhead,
　The wood-cat with eyes red
Crawleth close by, with her lithe crimson tongue
　Licking her clumsy young,
And, deep within the open prairie nigh,
　Hawks swoop and struck birds cry!

Dark maiden, what is he thou lookest on?
　O ask not, but begone!
Go! for his eyes are blue, his skin is white,
　And giant-like his height.
To him thou wouldst appear a tiny thing,
　Some small bird on the wing,
Some small deer to be kill'd ere it could fly,
　Or to be *tamed*, and die!—

O look not, look not, in the hunter's face,
　　Thou maid of the red race,
He is a tame thing, thou art weak and wild,
　　Thou lovely forest-child !
How should the deer by the great deer-hound
　　walk,
　　The wood-dove seek the hawk,—
Away ! away ! lest he should wake from rest,
　　Fly, sun-bird, to thy nest.

Why doth she start, and backward softly creep ?
　　He stirreth in his sleep—
Why doth she steal away with wondering eyes ?
　　He stretches limbs, and sighs.
Peace ! she hath fled—and he is all alone,
　　While, with a yawn and groan
The man sits up, rubs eyelids, grips his gun,
　　Stares heavenward at the sun,
And cries aloud, stretching himself anew :
　　"*Broad day*,—by all that's blue ! "

EUREKA.

ON the shores of the Atlantic,
Where the surge rolls fierce and frantic,
Where the mad winds cry and wrestle
With each frail and bird-like vessel,—
Down in Maine, where human creatures
Are amphibious in their natures,
And the babies, sons or daughters,
Float like fishes in the waters,—
Down in Maine, by the Atlantic,
Grew the Harts, of race gigantic,
And the tallest and the strongest
Was Eureka Hart, the youngest.

Like a bear-cub as a baby,
Rough, and rear'd as roughly as may be,

He had rudely grown and thriven
Till, a giant, six foot seven,
Bold and ready for all comers,
He had reach'd full thirty summers.
All his brethren, thrifty farmers,
Had espoused their rural charmers,
Settling down once and for ever
By the Muskeosquash River:
Thrifty men, devout believers,
Of the tribe of human *beavers ;*
Life to them, with years increasing,
Was an instinct never-ceasing
To build dwellings multifarious
In the fashion called gregarious,
To be honest in their station,
And increase the population
Of the beavers ! They, moreover,
Tho' their days were cast in clover,
Had the instinct of *secreting ;*
Toiling hard while time was fleeting,

To lay by in secret places,
[Like the bee and squirrel races,]
Quiet stores of yellow money,
[Which is human nuts and honey.]

Tho' no flowers of dazzling beauty
In their ploughshare line of duty
Rose and bloom'd, still, rural daisies,
Such as every village raises,
From the thin soil of their spirits
Grew and throve.   Their gentle merits
Free of any gleam of passion,
Flower'd in an instructive fashion.
Quite convinced that life was fleeting
Every week they went to meeting,
Met and prayed to God in dozens,
Uncles, nephews, nieces, cousins,
Joining there in adoration,
All the beaver population!

From this family one creature,
Taller and more fair of feature,
Err'd and wander'd, slightly lacking
In the building, breeding, packing,
Tribal-instinct ; and would never
Settle down by wood or river,
Build a house or take a woman
In the pleasant fashion common
To his race ; evincing rather
Traces of some fiercer father,
Panther-like, to hunting given
In the eye of the blue heaven !
When beneath the mother's bosom
His great life began to blossom,
Haply round her winds were crying,
O'er her head the white clouds flying,
At her feet the wild waves flowing,
All things moving, coming, going,
And the motion and vibration
Reach'd the thing in embryoation,

On its unborn soul conferring
Endless impulse to be stirring,—
To be ever wandering, racing,
Bird-like, wave-like, chased or chasing!
Born beside the stormy ocean,
'Twas the giant's earliest notion
To go roaming on the billow,
With a damp plank for a pillow.
In his youth he went as sailor
With the skipper of a whaler;
But in later life he better
Loved to feel no sort of fetter,
All his own free pathway mapping
In the forest,—hunting, trapping.
By great rivers, thro' vast valleys,
As thro' some enchanted palace
Ever bright and ever changing,
Many years he went a-ranging,—
Free as any wave, and only
Lonely as a cloud is lonely,

C

Floating in a void, surveying
Endless tracts for endless straying.

Pause a minute and regard him!
Years of hardships have not marr'd him.
Limbs made perfect, iron-solder'd,
Narrow-hipp'd and mighty-shoulder'd,
Whisker'd, bearded, strong and stately,
With a smile that lurks sedately
In still eyes of a cold azure,
Never lighting to sheer pleasure,
Stands he there, 'mid the green trees
Like the Greek god, Herakles.

Stay, nor let the bright allusion
Lead your spirit to confusion.
Tho' a wanderer, and a creature
Almost as a god in feature,
This man's nature was as surely
Soulless and instinctive purely,

As the natures of those others,
His sedater beaver-brothers;
Nothing brilliant, bright, or frantic,
Nothing maidens style romantic,
Flash'd his slow brain morn or night
Into spiritual light!

As waves run, and as clouds wander,
With small power to feel or ponder,
Roam'd this thing in human clothing,
Intellectually—nothing!
Further in his soul receding,
Certain signs of beaver-breeding
Kept his homely wits in see-saw;
Part was Jacob, part was Esau;
No revolter; a believer
In the dull creed of the beaver;
Strictly moral; seeing beauty
In the ploughshare line of duty;

Loving nature as beasts love it,
Eating, drinking, tasting of it,
With no wild poetic gleaming,
Seldom shaping, never dreaming;
Beaver with a wandering craze,
Walked Eureka in God's ways.

Now ye know him, now ye see him;
Nought from beaver-blood can free him;
Yet stand by and shrewdly con him,
While a wild light strikes upon him,
While a gleam of glory finds him,
Flashes in his eyes and blinds him,
Shapes his mind to its full measure,
Raising him, in one mad pleasure,
'Spite the duller brain's control,
To the stature of a SOUL!

III

THE CAPTURE.

THE wild wood rings, the wild wood gleams,
  The wild wood laughs with echoes gay;
Thro' its green heart a bright beck streams,
Sparkling like gold in the sun's beams,
  But creeping, like a silvern ray,
  Where hanging boughs make dim the day.
Hush'd, hot, and Eden-like all seems,
And onward thro' the place of dreams
  Eureka Hart doth stray.

Strong, broad-awake, and happy-eyed,
With the loose tangled light for guide,
He wanders, and at times doth pass
Thro' open glades of gleaming grass,

With spiderwort and larkspur spread,
And great anemones blood-red;
On every side the forest closes,
  The myriad trees are interlaced,
Starr'd with the white magnolia roses,
  And by the purple vines embraced.
Beneath on every pathway shine
The fallen needles of the pine;
Around are dusky scented bowers,
Bridged with the glorious lian-flowers.
Above, far up thro' the green trees,
  The palm thrusts out its fan of green,
Which softly stirs in a soft breeze,
  Far up against the heavenly sheen.

And all beneath the topmost palm
Is sultry shade and air of balm,
Where, shaded from the burning rays,
Scream choirs of parroquets and jays;

Where in the dusk of dream is heard
The shrill cry of the echo-bird;
And on the grass, as thick as bees,
   Run mocking birds and wood-doves small
Pecking the blood-red strawberries,
   And fruits that from the branches fall:
All rising up with gleam and cry,
When the bright snake glides hissing by,
Springs from the grass, and, swift as light,
Slips after the cameleons bright
From bough to bough, and here and there
Pauses and hangs in the green air,
Festoon'd in many a glistening fold,
Like some loose chain of gems and gold.

Smoke from a mortal pipe is blent
With cedar and acacia scent:
Phlegmatically relishing,
   Eureka smokes; from every tree

The wood-doves brood, the sun-birds sing,
The forest doth salute its King,
    The monarch Man,—but what cares he?
His eyes are dull, his soul in vain
Hears the strange tongues of his domain,
No echo comes to the soft strain
From the dull cavern of his brain.

But hark! what quick and sparkling cry
Darts like a fountain to the sky?
How, human voices! strangely clear,
They burst upon the wanderer's ear.
He stops, he listens—hark again,
Wild rippling laughter rises plain!

O'er his fair face a look of wonder
Is spreading—" Injins here—by thunder!"
    He cocks his gun, and stands to hear,

Sets his white teeth together tight,
   Then, silent-footed as the deer,
Creeps to the sound.   The branches bright
Thicken around him; with quick flight
The doves and blue-birds gleam away,
Shooting in showers from spray to spray.
A thicket of a thousand blooms,
   Green, rose, white, blue, one rainbow glow,
Closes around him; strange perfumes,
Crush'd underfoot in the rich glooms,
   Loads the rich air as he doth go;
   The harmless snakes around him glow
With emerald eyes; lithe arms of vine
Trip him and round his neck entwine,
Bursting against his stained skin
Their grapes of purple glossy-thin.
But still the rippling laughter flows
Before him as he creeps and goes,
Till suddenly, with a strange look,
He crouches down in a green nook,

Crouches and gazes from the bowers,
Curtain'd and cover'd up in flowers.

O, what strange sight before him lies?
Why doth he gaze with sparkling eyes
And beating heart?   Deep, bright, and cool,
Before him gleams a crystal pool,
Fed by the beck: and o'er its brim
Festoons of roses mirror'd dim
Hang drooping low on every side;
    And glorious moths and dragon flies
Hover above, and gleaming-eyed
    The stingless snake hangs blossom-wise,
In loose folds sleeping.   Not on these
Gazes Eureka thro' the trees:
Snake never made such smiles to grace
His still blue eyes and sun-tann'd face,
And never flower, howe'er so fair,
Would fix that face to such a stare.

And yet like gleaming water-snakes
  They wind and wanton in the pool.
Above their waists in flickering flakes
The molten sunlight slips and shakes ;
  Beneath, their gleaming limbs bathe cool.
One floats above with laughter sweet,
And splashes silver with her feet ;
One clinging to the drooping boughs
  Leans back, and lets her silken hair
Rain backward from her rippling brows,
  While on her shoulders dark and bare
  Blossoms fall thick and linger there
Nestling and clinging. To the throat
Cover'd, one dark-eyed thing doth float,
Her face a flower, her locks all wet,
Tendrils and leaves around it set ;
O sight most strangely beautiful,
Three Indian naïads in a pool !

Eureka, be it understood,
Though beaver-born, is flesh and blood,

And what he saw in day's broad gold
Was stranger far a thousand fold,
Than that wild scene bold Tam O'Shanter
   In Scotland saw one winter night,
(Ah with the Scottish Bard to canter,
On Pegasus to Fame instanter,
   Singing one song so trim and tight !)
He look'd, and look'd, like Tam ; like him,
On the most fair of face and limb
Fixing most long his wondering eye ;
For I like greater bards should lie,
If I averr'd that all and one
Who sported there beneath the sun,
Were gloriously fair of face ;
But they were women of red race,
Clad in the most bewitching dress,
Their own unconscious loveliness ;
And tho' their beauty might not be
   Perfect and flawless, they were fine,
Bright-eyed, red-lipp'd, made strong and free

In many a cunning curve and line
  A sculptor would have deem'd divine.
Not so the rest, who all around
With fierce eyes squatted on the ground,
Nodding approval :—squaws and crones
Clapping their hands with eager groans.
These were the witches, I might say,
Of this new tropic Alloway.
[As for the Devil—even *he*
  Was by the Serpent represented
Swinging asleep from a green tree,—
  Reflected, gloriously painted,
In the bright water where the three
Laugh'd and disported merrily.]

But chiefly poor Éureka gazed,
Trembling, dumb-stricken, and amazed,
On the most beautiful of all,
  Who standing on the water-side,
A perfect shape queenly and tall
  Stood in the sun erect, and dried

Her gleaming body head to feet
In one broad ray of golden heat.
Naked she stood, but her strange sheen
Of beauty clad her like a queen,
And beaming rings of yellow gold
Were round her wrists and ankles roll'd,
And on her skin Eureka scann'd
A symbol bright as of a brand
Held burning in a human hand.

Smiling, she spake in a strange tongue,
And eager laughter round her rung,
While wading out all lustrous-eyed
She sat upon the water side,
And pelted merrily the rest
With blossoms bright and flowers of jest.

Ah, little did Eureka guess,
While wondering at her loveliness,

The same fair form had softly crept
And look'd upon him while he slept,
And thought him (*him!* the man of Maine!
Civilizee with beaver-brain!)
Beauteous, in passion's first wild beam,
Beyond all Indian guess or dream!

Eureka Hart, though tempted more
Than e'er was mortal man before,
Did not like Tam O'Shanter break
   The charm with mad applause or call;
Too wise for such a boor's mistake,
   He held his tongue, observing all;
But while the hunter forward leant,
Sharing the glorious merriment,
He moved a little unaware
   The better to behold the sport,
And lo! upon the heavy air
   Off went his gun with sharp report,

And while the bullet past his ear
   Whizz'd quick, he stagger'd with the shock,
And with one scream distinct and clear
   Rose the red women in a flock.
The naked bathers stood and scream'd,
The brown squaws cried, their white teeth
      gleam'd;
And ere he knew, with startled face
He stagger'd to the open space;
The sharp vines tript him, and, confounded,
   He stumbled, grasping still his gun,—
And, by the chattering choir surrounded,
   Half dazed, lay lengthways in the sun.

As when a clumsy grizzly bear
Breaks on a dove-cot unaware,
As when some snake, unwieldy heap,
Drops from a pine-bough, half asleep,
Plump in the midst of grazing sheep;—
Even so into the women-swarm
Suddenly fell the giant's form!

They leapt, they scream'd, they closed, they
    scatter'd,

Some fled, some stood, all call'd and chatter'd,

And to the man in his amaze

Innumerable seem'd as jays

And parroquets in the green ways.

Had they been men, despite their throng,

In sooth he had lain still less long;

But somehow in the stars 'twas fated,

He for a space was *fascinated !*

And ere he knew what he should do,

All round about him swarm'd the crew,

Sharp-eyed, quick-finger'd, and, despite

His struggling, clung around him tight;

Half choked, half smother'd by embraces,

In a wild mist of arms and faces,

He stagger'd up; in vain, in vain!

Hags, squaws, and maidens in a chain

Clung round him, and with quicker speed

Than ye this running rhyme can read,

With tendrils tough as thong of hide,
Torn from the trees on every side,
In spite of all his strength, the band
Had bound the Giant foot and hand.

IV.

THRO' THE WOOD.

THROUGH the gleaming forest closes,
Where on white magnolia-roses
Light the dim-draped queen reposes,
  Lo, they lead the captive giant.

Shrieking shrill as jays around him,
They have led him, they have bound him,
With a wreath of vine-leaves crown'd him,
  Which he weareth, half defiant.

If their ears could hear him swearing!
Of his oaths he is not sparing,
While, with hands sharp-claw'd for tearing,
  Hags and beldams burn to rend him.

If the younger, prettier creatures
Heard that tallest of beseechers,
While he pleads with frantic features!
　But they do *not* comprehend him.

In their Indian tongue they're crying,
From the forest multiplying,
Mocking, murmuring, leaping, flying,
　While he shouts out, "D—— the women!"

All his mighty strength is nothing:
Like a ship, despite his loathing,
Mid these women scant of clothing
　He is tossing, struggling, screaming.

Crown'd like Bacchus on he passes,
O'er deep runlets, through great grasses,
While [like flies around molasses]
　Fair and foul are round him humming!

Half a day they westward wander,
Stopping not to rest or ponder;
Then the forest ends; and yonder
   Wild dogs bark to hear them coming.

Cluster'd in an open clearing
Stand the wigwams they are nearing,
Bark the dogs, a strange foot fearing,
   Low the cattle,—straight before them.

Out into the sunlight leaping,
There they see the wigwams sleeping,
With a blue smoke upward creeping,
   And the burning azure o'er them!

All is still, save for the screaming
Children from the wigwams streaming,
All is still and sweet to seeming,
   Not a man's face forward thrusting.

Thinks Eureka, "This looks stranger—
Ne'er a man—then double danger;
Many a year I've been a ranger,—
  Woman's mercy put no trust in!"

As he speaks in trepidation,
All his heart in palpitation,
He is fill'd with admiration
  At a vision wonder-laden.

From the largest wigwam, slowly,
While the women-band bow lowly,
Comes an old man white and holy,
  Guided gently by a maiden!

V

THE RED TRIBE.

NINETY long years had slowly shed
Their snows upon the patriarch's head,
And on a staff of ash he leant,
Shaking and bending as he went.
His face, sepulchral, long, and thin,
Was shrivell'd like a dried snake's skin,
And on the cheeks and forehead dark
Tattoo'd was many a livid mark,
And in the midst his eyeballs white
Roll'd blankly, seeing not the light;
And when he listen'd in his place

   You saw at once that he was *blind*,
For with a visionary grace

   Dim mem'ries moved from his own mind,

And the wild waters of his face
  Waved in a wondrous wind.

From an artistic point of sight,
The aged man was faultless quite;
Albeit, the raiment he did wear
  Was somewhat hybrid; for example,
A pair of pantaloons threadbare
Match'd strangely with his Indian air,
  And blanket richly wrought and ample;
And, though perchance not over clean,
He had a certain gentle mien
Kindly and kingly; and a smile
Complacent in the kingly style,
Yet fraught with strangely subtle rays,
The lingering light of other days :—
Brightness and motion such as we
Trace in the trouble of the Sea,
When the long stormy day is sped,
And in the last light dusky-red

The waves are sinking, one by one.

But she who led him!—In the sun
She gleam'd beside him, like a rose
That by a dark sad water grows
And trembles. In a moment's space
Eureka recognised the face!
'Twas hers, who stood most beautiful,
Queen of those bathers in the pool!
But her bright locks were braided now
Around her clear and glistening brow,
And on her limbs she wore a dress
Less rich than her own loveliness.
From the artistic point of view,
The maiden's dress was faultless too,
But, look'd at closely, not so rare
As white-skinn'd maid would wish to wear ;
'Twas coarsest serge of sullen dye,
Albeit embroider'd curiously ;

And the few ornaments she wore
Were trifles valueless and poor ;—
Their merit, let us straight confess,
And all the merit of her dress,
Was that they form'd for eyes to see
Nimbus enough of drapery
And ornament, just to suggest
The costume that became her best—
Her own brave beauty.   She just wore
Enough for modesty—no more.
She was not, as white beauties seem,
Smother'd, like strawberries in cream,
With folds of silk and linen.   No!
The Indians wrap their babies so,
And *we* our women ; who, alas!
Waddle about upon the grass,
Distorted, shapeless, smother'd, choking,
Hideous, and horribly provoking,
Because we long, without offence,
To tear the mummy-wrappings thence,

And show the human form enchanting
That 'neath the fatal folds is panting !

She was a shapely creature, tall,
And slightly form'd, but plump withal,—
Shapely as deers are—finely fair
As creatures nourish'd by warm air,
And luscious fruits that interfuse
Something of their own glorious hues,
And the rich odour that perfumes them,
Into the body that consumes them.
She had drank richness thro' and thro'
As the great flowers drink light and dew ;
And she had caught from wandering streams
Their restless motion ; and strange gleams
From snakes and flowers that glow'd around
Had stolen into her blood, and found
Warmth, peace, and silence ; and, in brief,
Her looks were bright beyond belief

Of those who meet in the green ways
The rum-wreck'd squaws of later days.

[I would be accurate, nor essay
Again in Cooper's pleasant way
A picture highly wrought and splendid
Of the red race whose pride has ended.
Nor here by contrast err : indeed,
The red man is of Esau's seed,
Hath Esau's swiftness, and, I guess,
Much, too, of Esau's loveliness.
A thousand years in the free wild
He fought and hunted, leapt and smiled ;
A million impulses and rays
Shot thro' his spirit's tangled ways,
Working within his dusky frame
As in a storm-cloud worketh flame,
Shaping his strength as years did roll
Into the semblance of his soul.

Slowly his shape and spirit caught
The living likeness wonder-fraught,
The golden, many-coloured moods
Of those free plains and pathless woods ;
Those blooms that burst, those streams that run
One changeless rainbow in the sun !
Unto the hues of this rich clime
His nature was subdued in time ;
And he became as years increased
A glorious animal, at least.]

Soon like a mist did disappear
Eureka Hart's first foolish fear,
For courteously the chief address'd him,
  In English speech distinct tho' broken,
Bade them unloose and cease to pest him,
  And further, smiling and soft spoken,
Inquired his country and his name,
Whither he fared and whence he came.

Eureka, from the withes released,
Shook himself like a bright-eyed beast,
And mutter'd; then, meeting the look
Of that bright naïad of the brook,
Blush'd like a shamefaced boy, while she
Stood gazing on him silently,
With melancholy orbs whose flame
Confused his soul with secret shame.

In a brief answer and explicit,
He told the cause of his strange visit.
The old chief smiled and whisper'd low
   Into the small ear of the maiden :
Her large eyes fell, and with a glow
   Of dark, deep rose her face was laden.
Then, like a sound of many waters,
Innumerable screams and chatters,
The voices of the women-band
   Broke out in passion and in power ;

But, at the raising of his hand,
  Ceased, like the swift cease of a shower.

Full soon Eureka saw and knew
That the Dark Dame who favours few
Had brought him to a friendly place,
Where, far from cities, a mild race
Of happy Indians spent their days
'Mid pastures and well-water'd ways.
An ancient people strong and good,
With something sacred in their blood;
Scatter'd and few, to strangers kind;
Wise in the ways of rain and wind;
Peaceful when pleased, bloody when roused,
They dwelt there comfortably housed;
And in those gardens ever fair,
Hunted and fish'd with little care.
Just then their braves were roaming bound
On an adjacent hunting-ground;

And all the population then
Were women wild and aged men.—
But he, that old man blind and tall,
Was a great King, and Chief of all ;
And she who led him was by birth
His grandchild, dearest thing on earth
To his dusk age ; and dear tenfold
    Because no other kin had she,—
Since sire and mother both lay cold
    Under Death's leafless Upas-tree.

Enough ! here faltereth my first song ;
    Eureka, still in secret captured,
In that lost Eden lingers long,
    And his big bosom beats enraptured.
Long days and nights speed o'er him there ;
What binds him *now ?* a woman's hair !
What doth he see ? a woman's eyes
Above him luminously rise !

What doth he kiss? a woman's mouth
Sweeter than spice-winds of the south!
By golden streams he lies full blest,
And Red Rose blossoms on his breast.

O love! love! love! whose spells are shed
On bodies black, white, yellow, red—
Flame of all matter,—flower of clay,—
Star of pangenesis;—but stay!
A theme of so divine a tone
Must have a canto of its own!

Part II.

RED ROSE.

I

ERYCINA RIDENS.

O LOVE! O spirit of being!
  O wonderful secret of breath,
Sweeter than hearing or seeing,
  Sadder than sorrow or death.

Earth with its holiest flavour,
  Life with its lordliest dower,
The fruit's strange essence and flavour,
  Bloom and scent of the flower.

[Thus might a modern poet,
  O Aphrodite, uptake
His fanciful flute and blow it,
  And wail the echoes awake!]

O love, love, Aphrodite,
   Cytherea divine,
I hold you fever'd and flighty,
   And seek a pleasanter shrine.

Yet hither, O spirit fervent,
   Just to help me along,
Forget I am not thy servant,
   And blow in the sails of my song.

For lo ! 'tis a situation
   Caused by thyself, 'twould seem ;
The old, old foolish sensation,
   Two lovers lost in a dream.

O the wonder and glory,
   Bright as Creation's burst !
O the ancestral story,
   Old as Adam the first !

Flame, and fervour, and fever,
  Flashing from morning to night,
Alliteration for ever
  Of love, and longing, and light.

How should the story vary?
  How should the song be new?
Music and meaning marry?
  'Tis love, love, love, all thro'!

As it was in the beginning,
  Is, and ever shall be!
Loving, and love for the winning,
  Love, and the soul set free.

[An invocation like this is
  Need not be over wise;
Who shall interpret kisses?
  What is the language of eyes?]

Again a man and a woman
   Feeling the old blest thing,
Better than voices human
   A bird on the bough could sing.

Only a sound is wanted,
   Merry, and happy, and loud,—
Such as the lark hath panted
   Up in the golden cloud.

Lips, and lips to kiss them ;
   Eyes, and eyes to behold ;
Hands, and hands to press them ;
   Arms, and arms to enfold.

The love that comes to the palace,
   That comes to the cottage door ;
The ever-abundant chalice
   Brimming for rich and poor;

The love that waits for the winning,
　The love that ever is free,
That was in the world's beginning,
　Is, and ever shall be!

II

LOG AND SUNBEAM.

As a pine-log prostrate lying,
   Slowly thro' its knotted skin
Feels the warm revivifying
   Spring-time thrill and tremble in;
As a pine-log, strong and massive,
Feels the light and lieth passive,
While a Sunbeam, coming daily,
Creeps upon its bosom gaily;
Warms the bark with quick pulsations,
Warms and waits each day in patience,
While the green begins to brighten,
And the sap begins to heighten,—

Till at last from its hard bosom
Suddenly there slips a blossom
Green as emerald!—then another!
   Then a third! then more and more!
Till the soft green bud-knots smother
   What was sapless wood before;
Till the thing is consecrated
   To the spirit of the Spring,
Till the love for all things fated
   Burns and beautifies the thing ;—
And the wood-doves sit and con it,
   And the squirrels from on high
Fluttering drop their nuts upon it,
   And the bee and butterfly
Find it pleasant to alight there,
And taps busy morn and night there
   Many a bird with golden beak;
Till, since all has grown so bright there,
   It would cry (if Logs could speak),
" Sunbeam, sunbeam, I'm your debtor!
   I was fit for firewood nearly.

I'm considerably better,
   And I *love* you, Sunbeam, dearly!"

. . . *Thou*, Eureka, wast the wood!
   She, the Sunbeam of the Spring,
Vivifying thy dull blood
   Past thy mind's imagining!
Till the passion of her loving,
   Seething forth with ardours frantic,
Brought the buds forth, set thee moving,
   Made thee almost look romantic.

"O would some power the giftie gie us
To see oursels as others see us!"
   Sang the wise ploughman in his power.
And yet, Eureka, had sweet Heaven
To thee her wondrous "giftie" given
   To see thyself as seen that hour,
To know thy features as *she* knew them,
   To see thy shape as *she* perceived it;

To see thine eyes, and thro' and thro' them,
  Into thy Soul as she conceived it;
Either thy blood had run mad races,
  And driven thee to some maniac action;
Or (what more likely in the case is)
  Thy wits had frozen to stupefaction!

For never god in olden story,
  When the gods had honour due,
Gather'd brighter guise and glory,
  In an adoring mortal's view.
Let me own it, though thy nature
  Was sedate and beaver-bred,
As a god thou wert in stature,
  Fair of face and proud of tread;
And thine eyes were luminous glasses,
  And thy face a glorious scroll,
And the radiant light that passes
O'er the dumb flowers and the grasses,
  Caught thy gaze and *look'd* like Soul;

And the animal vibration
  Throbbing in thee at her touch,
The wild earthly exaltation,
  Beasts and birds can feel as much,
Radiating and illuming
  Every fibre of thy flesh,
Made thee beautiful and blooming,
  Great and glorious, fair and fresh ;
Fit it seem'd for love to yearn to,
  For a fairer Soul than thine,
Morning, noon, and night to burn to,
  In a flash that felt divine.
Her tall white chief, whom God had brought her
From the far-off Big-Sea Water !
Her warrior of the pale races,
With wise tongues and paintless faces ;
More than mortal, a great creature,
Soft of tongue, and fine of feature ;
As the wind that blew above her
  O'er the hunting-fields of azure,

As the stately clouds that hover
   In the air that pants for pleasure,
Full of strength and motion stately,
   Were thy face and form unto her;
And thy blue eyes pleased her greatly,
   And thy clear voice trembled thro' her;
And for minute after minute
   She did pore upon thy face,
Read the lines and guess within it
   The great spirit of thy race;
And thou seemedst altogether
   A great creature, fair of skin,
Born in scenes of softer weather,
   Nobler than her savage kin !

As a peasant maiden homely
   Might regard some lordly wooer,
Find each feature trebly comely
   From the pride it stoops unto her;

Thus, Eureka, she esteem'd thee
   Fairer for thy finer blood ;
She revered thee, loved thee, deem'd thee
   Wholly beautiful and good !
And her day-dream ne'er was broken,
   As some mortal day-dreams are,
By a word or sentence spoken
   In thy coarse vernacular.
For she could not speak a dozen
   Words as used by the white nation !
And thy speech seem'd finely chosen,
   Since she made her own translation,
Scarce a syllable quite catching,
   Yet, upon thy bosom leaning,
Out of every sentence snatching
   Music with its own sweet meaning.

Powers above ! the situation's
   Psychological, I swear !

How express the false relations
   Of this strange-assorted pair?
Happy, glorious, self-deluded,
On the handsome face she brooded,
Ne'er by word or gesture driven
From her day-dream sweet as heaven.
In her native language for him
   She had warrior's names most sweet:
And she loved and did adore him,
   Falling fawn-like at his feet;
More, the rapturous exultation
   Struck *him!* blinded *him*, in turn!
Till with passionate sensation
   Body and brain began to burn;—
And he yielded to the bursting,
Burning, blinding, hungering, thirsting,
   Passion felt by beasts and men!
And his eyes caught love and rapture,
And he held her close in capture,
   Kissing lips—that kiss'd again!

F

III.

NUPTIAL SONG.

WHERE were they wedded? In no Temple of ice
    Built up by human fingers;
The floor was strewn with flowers of fair device,
    The wood-birds were the singers.

Who was the Priest? The priest was the still
    Soul,
    Calm, gentle, and low-spoken;
He read a running brooklet like a scroll,
    And trembled at the token.

What was the service? 'Twas the service read
    When Adam's faith was plighted!

The tongue was silent, but the lips rose-red
  In silence were united.

Who saw it done? The million starry eyes
  Of one ecstatic Heaven.
Who shared the joy? The flowers, the trees,
    the skies
  Thrill'd as each kiss was given.

Who was the Bride? A spirit strong and true,
  Beauteous to human seeing,—
Soft elements of flesh, air, fire, and dew,
  Blent in one Rose of being.

What was her consecration? Innocence! ·
  Pure as the wood doves round her,
Nothing she knew of rites—the strength in-
    tense
  Of God and Nature found her.

As freely as maids give a lock away,
  She gave herself unto him.
What was the Bridegroom? Clay, and common
    clay,
  Yet the wild joy slipt through him.

Hymen, O Hymen! By the birds was shed
  A matrimonial cadence!
Da nuces! Squirrels strew'd the nuts, instead
  Of rosy youths and maidens!

Eureka, yea, Eureka was to blame—
  He was an erring creature:
Uncivilised by one wild flash of flame
  He waver'd back on Nature.

He kiss'd her lips, he drank her breath in bliss,
  He drew her to his bosom:
As a clod kindles at the Spring's first kiss
  His being burst to blossom!

Who rung the bells? The breeze, the merry breeze,
    Set all in bright vibration:
Clear, sweet, yet low, there trembled through the trees
    The nuptial jubilation!

IV.

ARRÊTEZ!

O'ER this joy I dare not linger :
Stands a Shape with lifted finger
Crying in a low voice, " Singer!
    Far too much of Eve and Adam.

" Details of this dark connection
I desire not for inspection !"
And the Bard, with genuflexion,
    Answers, "I obey thee, Madam !"

Stands the Moral Shape reproving,
While I linger o'er this loving ;
Cries the voice, " Pass on ! be moving!
    We are virtuous, here to nor'ward !"

Constable, I force cessation
To my flood of inspiration ;
Such a theme for adumbration !
    I resign it, and move forward.

V.

THE FAREWELL.

Love, O love! thou bright and burning
Weathercock for ever turning;
Gilded vane, fix'd for our seeing
On the highest spire of being;
Symbol, indication; reeling
Round to every wind of feeling;
Only pointing some sad morrow,
In one sudden gust of sorrow,
Sunset-ward, where redly, slowly,
Passion sets in melancholy.

In the wood-ways, roof'd by heaven,
Were the nuptial kisses given;

In the dark green, moonbeam-haunted
Forest; in the bowers enchanted
Where the fiery specks are flying,
And the whip-poor-will is crying;
Where the heaven's open blue eye
Thro' the boughs broods dark and dewy,
And the white magnolia glimmers
Back the light in starry tremors;
Where the acacia in the shady
Silence trembles like a lady
Scented sweet and softly breathing;
There, amid the brightly wreathing,
Blooming branches, did they capture
Love's first consecrated rapture.

Pure she came to him, a maiden
Innocent as Eve in Eden,
Tho' in secret; for she dreaded
Wrath of kinsmen tiger-headed,
In whose vision, fierce and awful,
Love for white men was unlawful.

Yet in this her simple reason
Knew no darker touch of treason
Than dost thou, O white and dainty
English maid of sweet-and-twenty,
When from guardian, father, brother,
[Harsh protectors, one or t'other,]
Off you trip, self-handed over
To your chosen lord and lover,
Tears of love and rapture shedding
In the hush of secret wedding.

Now from these lost days Elysian,
Modestly I drop my vision!
Rose the wave supreme and splendid,
To a tremulous crest, and ended,
Falling, falling, one sad morrow,
In a starry spray of sorrow.

Whether 'twas by days or hours,
Weeks or months, in those bright bowers,

They their gladness counted,—whether
Like the one day's summer weather
At the pole, their bliss upstarted,
Brighten'd, blacken'd, and departed,—
I relate not; all my story
Is, that soon or late this glory
Fell and faded.   After daylight
Came an eve of sad and gray light;
There were tears—wild words were spoken,
Down the cup was dash'd, and broken.

First came danger,—eyeballs fiery
Watch'd the pair in fierce inquiry;
Secret footsteps dodged the lovers;
As a black hawk slowly hovers
O'er the spot amid the heather
Where the gray birds crouch together,
Hung Suspicion o'er the places
Where they sat with flaming faces.

Next came—what d'ye call the dreary
Heavy-hearted thing and weary,
In old weeds of joy bedizen'd?
By the shallow French 'tis christen'd
Ennui !   Ay, the snake that grovels
In a host of scrofulous novels,
Leper even of the leprous
Race of serpents vain and viprous,
Bred of slimy eggs of evil,
Sat on by the printer's devil,
Last, to gladden absinthe-lovers,
Born by broods in paper covers!

After the great wave of madness,
Ennui came ; and tho' in gladness
Still the Indian maiden's nature
Clung round the inferior creature,
Though with burning, unconsuming,
Deathless love *her* heart was blooming,

He grew weary, and his passion
In a dull evaporation
Slowly lessen'd, till caressing
Grew distracting and distressing.
Conscience waken'd in a fever,
Just a day too late, as ever;
He remember'd, one fine day,
His relations far away.

All the beavers! the deceiver!
After all, he *was* a beaver
Born and bred, tho' the unchanging
Dash of wild blood kept him ranging;
Beaver-conscience, now awaken'd,
Since the first true bliss had slacken'd,
Whisper'd with a sad affection,
"Fie! it is a strange connection!
Is it worthy? Can it profit?
Sits the world approving of it?"
While another whisper said,
"*You*'re a white man! She is red!"

Ne'ertheless he seem'd to love her,
Watch'd her face and bent above her,
Fondly thinking, " Now, I wonder
If the world would blame my blunder?
If her skin were only whiter,
If her manners were politer,
I would take her with me nor'ward,
Wed her, cling to her thenceforward,
Clothe her further, just a tittle,
Live respectable and settle!"
She was silent, as he brooded
Handsome-faced and beaver-mooded,
Thinking, "Now my chief is seeming
Where the fires of fight are streaming!
O, how great and grand his face is,
Lit with light of the pale races!"
And she bent her brows before him,
Kiss'd his hands, and did adore him,
And she waited in deep duty;
While her eyes of dazzling beauty,

Like two jewels ever streaming
  Broken yet unceasing rays,
Watch'd him as in beaver-dreaming
  He would walk in the green ways.

Still he seem'd to her a splendid
Creature, but his trance had ended ;
More and more, thro' ever seeing
  Red skins round him, he lost patience,
More and more the hybrid being
  Sigh'd for civilised relations ;
For Eureka Hart, tho' wholly
  Of a common social mind,
Narrow-natured, melancholy,
  Hated *ties* of any kind ;—
Yet if any tie could hold him
  To a place or to a woman,
'Twould be one the world had told him
  Was respectable and common.

Here, then, hemm'd in by a double
Dark dilemma, he found trouble,
And with look a Grecian painter
   Would have given to a god,
Feeling passion still grow fainter,
   Thought, "I reckon things look odd!
Wouldn't Parson Pendon frown,
If he knew, in Drowsietown?"

As he spoke he saw the village
Rising up with tilth and tillage,
Saw the smithy, like an eye
Flaming bloodshot at the sky,
Saw the sleepy river flowing,
   Saw the swamps burn in the sun,
Saw the people coming, going,
   All familiar, one by one.
"There the plump old Parson goes,
Silver buckles on his toes,

Broad-brimm'd beaver on his head,
Clean-shaved chin, and cheek as red
As ripe pippins, kept in hay,
Polish'd on Thanksgiving day;
Black coat, breeches, all complete,
On the old mare he keeps his seat,
Jogging on with smiles so bright
To creation left and right.
There's the Widow Abner smiling
  At her door as he goes past,
Guess she thinks she looks beguiling,
  But he cuts along more fast.
There's Abe Sinker drunk as ever,
  There's the pigs all in the gutter,
There's the miller by the river,
  Broad as long and fat as butter.
See it all, so plain and pleasant,
  Just like life their shadows pass,
Wonder how they are at present?
  Guess they think *I*'m gone to grass!"

While this scene he contemplated,
  Sighing like a homeless creature,
Round him, brightly concentrated,
  Glow'd the primal fire of Nature!
Rainbow-hued and rapturous-colour'd,
  With one burning brilliant look
Flaming fix'd upon the dullard,
  Nature rose in wild rebuke!
Shower'd her blossoms round him, o'er him,
  Breathed warm breath upon his face,
Flash'd her flowers and fruits before him,
  Follow'd him from place to place;
With wild jasmine and with amber
She perfumed his sleeping chamber,
Hung around him happy hours
With her arms of lustre-flowers,
Held to his in blest reposes
Her warm breasts of living roses;
Bade a thousand dazzling, crying,
  Living, creatures do him honour,
Stood herself, naked and sighing,

With an aureole upon her;
Then, with finger flashing brightly
   Pointing to her prime creation,—
Fruits and flowers and scents blent lightly
   In one dazzling adumbration,—
Cried unto him over and over,
"See my child! O love her, love her!
I eternal am, no comer
In a feeble flush of summer,
Like the hectic colour flying
Of a maid love-sick and dying;
Here no change, but ever burning
Quenchless fire, and ceaseless yearning :
Endless exquisite vibration
   Sweet as love's first nuptial kiss,
One soft sob of strange sensation
   Flowering into shapes of bliss;
And the brightest, O behold her
   With a changeless warmth like mine—
Love her! In thy soul enfold her!

Blend with *us*, and be divine!"
All in vain that fond entreating!
   Still Eureka's beaver-brain
Thought—"This climate's rather heating—
   Weather's cooler up in Maine!"

Yet no wonder Nature loved him,
   Sought to take his soul by storm,
Gloried when her meaning moved him,
   Clung in fondness round his form ;
For, in sooth, tho' unimpassion'd,
Gloriously the man was fashion'd :
One around whose strength and splendour
   Women would have pray'd to twine,
As the lian loves to blend her
   Being with the beech or pine.
And his smile when she was present
   Was seraphic, full of spirit,
And his voice was low and pleasant,
   And her soul grew bright to hear it!

And when tall he strode to meet her,
And his handsome face grew sweeter,
In her soul she thought, " O being,
Fair and gracious and deep-seeing,
White man, great man, far above me,
What am *I*, that thou shouldst love me ? "

She had learnt him with lips burning
(O for such a course of learning !)
Something of her speech,—'twas certain
Quite enough to woo and flirt in ;
Words not easy of translation
They transfused into sensation,
Soon discovering and proving,
   As a small experience teaches,
" Bliss " and " kiss," and other loving
   Words, are common to *all* speeches !
Ah, the rapture ! ah, the fleeting
Follies of each fond, mad meeting !

Smiling with red lips asunder,
Clapping hands at each fond blunder,
She instructed him right gaily
In her Indian *patois* daily.
Sweetly from his lips it sounded,
  Help'd with those great azure eyes,
Till upon his heart she bounded
  Panting praise with laughs and cries.
'Twas a speech antique and olden,
  Full of gurgling notes, it ran
Like some river rippling golden
  Down a dale Arcadian ;
Like the voices of doves brooding ;
  Like a fountain's gentle moan ;
Nothing commonplace intruding
  On its regal monotone :
Sounds and symbols interblending
  Like the heave of loving bosoms ;
Consonants like strong boughs bending,
  Snowing vowels down like blossoms !

Faltering in this tongue, he told her,
   Sitting in a secret place,
While with bright head on his shoulder,
   Luminous-eyed, she watch'd his face,
How, tho' every hour grown fonder,
   Tho' his soul was still aflame,
Still, he sigh'd once more to wander
   To the clime from whence he came ;
Just once more to look upon it,
Just for one brief hour to con it,
Just to see his kin and others
   In the Town where they did dwell,
Just to say to his white brothers
   One farewell, a last farewell.
Then to hasten back unto her,
   And to live with her and die. . . .
Sharp as steel his speech stabb'd thro' her,
   Cold she sat without a cry,
On her heart her small hand pressing,
   Breathing like a bird in pain,

Silent, tho' he smiled caressing,
  Kiss'd, but kissing not again.

Then she waken'd, like one waking
From a trance, and with heart aching
Clung around him, as if dreading
  Lest some hand should snatch him thence!
Then, upon his bosom shedding
  Tears of ecstacy intense,
By her gods conjured him wildly
  Never, never to depart!
O how meekly, O how mildly,
  Answer'd back Eureka Hart!

But by slow degrees he coax'd her,
  Night by night, and day by day,
With such specious spells he hoax'd her
  That her first fear fled away.
Slow she yielded, still believing
  Not for long he'd leave her lonely;

For he told her, still deceiving,
   'Twas a *little journey* only.
Poor, dark bird! nought *then* knew she
Of this world's geography!

Troubled, shaken, half-demented,
Broken-hearted—she assented.
Since, by wind, and wave, and vapour,
   By the shapes of earth and skies;
By the white moon's ghostly taper,
   By the stars that like dead eyes
Watch it burning; by the mystic
   Motion of the winds and woods;
By all dark and cabalistic
   Shapes of tropic solitudes;
By the waters melancholy;
   By God's hunting-fields of blue;
By all things that she deem'd holy
   He had promised to be true!
Just to pay a flying visit

To connections close at hand,
　Then to haste with love undying
　　Back unto that happy land.
'Twas enough! the Maid assented,
　　Thinking sadly, in her pain,
" He will never be contented
　　Till he sees them once again.
Thither, thither let him wander;
　　When once more I feel his kiss,
His proud spirit will be fonder
　　Since my love hath granted this!"

" Go!" she cried, and her dark features
Kindled like a dying creature's,
And her heart rose, and her spirit
Cried as if for God to hear it—
Wildly in her arms she press'd him
　　To her bosom broken-hearted—
Call'd upon her gods, and blest him!
　　And Eureka Hart departed.

VI

THE PAPER.

Here should my second canto end—yet stay
Listen a little ere ye turn away.

By night they parted; and she cut by night
One large lock from his forehead, which with
    bright,
Warm lips she kiss'd; then kiss'd the lock of
    hair,
With one quick sob of passionate despair;
And he, with hand that shook a little now,
Still with that burning seal upon his brow,
While in that bitter agony they embraced,
He in her little hand a paper placed,

Whereon, at her fond prayer, he had writ plain,

"*Eureka Hart, Drowsietown, State of Maine.*"

"For," thought he, "I have promised soon or
    late

Hither to come again to her, my mate;

And I will keep my promise, sure, some day,

Unless I die or sicken by the way.

But no man knows what pathway he may
    tread,—

To-morrow—nay, ere dawn—I may be dead!

And she shall know, lest foul my fortune proves,

The name and country of the man she loves;

And since she wishes it, to cheer her heart,

It shall be written down ere I depart."

And so it was; and while his kiss thrill'd thro'
    her,

With that loved lock of hair he gave it to her.

Aye, so it was; for in the woods at dawn

He from his pouch had an old letter drawn,

One leaf of which was blank, and this he took,

And smiling at the woman's wondering look,

While quietly she murmur'd, " T'is a charm ! "

In hunter's fashion he had prick'd his arm,

And, having pen nor ink, had ta'en a spear

Of thorn for stylus, and in crimson clear,

His own heart's blood, had writ the words she
    sought.

And in that hour deep pity in him wrought,

And he believed that he his vows would keep,

Nor e'er be treacherous to a love so deep.

"See ! " said he, as the precious words he gave,

" Keep this upon thy bosom, and be brave.

As sure as that red blood belong'd to me,

I shall, if I live on, return to thee.

If death should find me while thou here dost
    wait,

Thou canst at least make question of my fate

Of any white man whose stray feet may fare

Down hither, showing him the words writ there."

All this he said to her with faltering voice
In broken Indian, and in words less choice;
And quite persuaded of his good intent,
Shoulder'd his gun with a gay heart, and went.

And in that paper, while her fast tears fell,
She wrapt the lock of hair she loved so well,
And thrust it on her heart; and with sick sight,
Watch'd his great figure fade into the night;
Then raised her hands to her wild gods, that sped
Above her in a whirlwind overhead,
And the pines rock'd in tempest, and her form
Bent broken with the breathing of the storm.

O little paper! Blurr'd with secret tears!
O blood-red charm! O thing of hopes and fears!
Between two worlds a link, so faint, so slight,
The two worlds of the red man and the white!
Lie on her heart and soothe her soul's sad pain!

" EUREKA HART, DROWSIETOWN, STATE OF
       MAINE."

Part III.

WHITE ROSE.

I.

DROWSIETOWN.

O so drowsy! In a daze
Sweating 'mid the golden haze,
With its smithy like an eye
Glaring bloodshot at the sky,
And its one white row of street
Carpetted so green and sweet,
And the loungers smoking still
Over gate and window-sill;
Nothing coming, nothing going,
Locusts grating, one cock crowing,
Few things moving up or down,
All things drowsy—Drowsietown !

Thro' the fields with sleepy gleam,
Drowsy, drowsy steals the stream,

H

Touching with its azure arms
Upland fields and peaceful farms,
Gliding with a twilight tide
Where the dark elms shade its side ;
Twining, pausing sweet and bright
Where the lilies sail so white ;
Winding in its sedgy hair
Meadow-sweet and iris fair ;
Humming as it hies along
Monotones of sleepy song ;
Deep and dimpled, bright nut-brown,
Flowing into Drowsietown.

Far as eye can see, around,
Upland fields and farms are found,
Floating prosperous and fair
In the mellow misty air :
Apple-orchards, blossoms blowing
Up above,—and clover growing

Red and scented round the knees
Of the old moss-silvered trees.
Hark! with drowsy deep refrain,
In the distance rolls a wain;
As its dull sound strikes the ear,
Other kindred sounds grow clear—
Drowsy all—the soft breeze blowing,
Locusts grating, one cock crowing,
Cries like voices in a dream
Far away amid the gleam,
Then the waggons rumbling down
Thro' the lanes to Drowsietown.

Drowsy? Yea!—but idle? Nay!
Slowly, surely, night and day,
Humming low, well greased with oil,
Turns the wheel of human toil.
Here no grating gruesome cry
Of spasmodic industry;

No rude clamour, mad and mean,
Of a horrible machine!
Strong yet peaceful, surely roll'd,
Winds the wheel that whirls the gold.
Year by year the rich rare land
Yields its stores to human hand—
Year by year the stream makes fat
Every field and meadow-flat—
Year by year the orchards fair
Gather glory from the air,
Redden, ripen, freshly fed,
Their bright balls of golden red.
Thus, most prosperous and strong,
Flows the stream of life along
Six slow days! wains come and go,
Wheat-fields ripen, squashes grow,
Cattle browse on hill and dale,
Milk foams sweetly in the pail,
Six days: on the seventh day,
Toil's low murmur dies away—

All is husht save drowsy din
Of the waggons rolling in,
Drawn amid the plenteous meads
By small fat and sleepy steeds.
Folk with faces fresh as fruit
Sit therein or trudge afoot,
Brightly drest for all to see,
In their seventh-day finery :
Farmers in their breeches tight,
Snowy cuffs, and buckles bright ;
Ancient dames and matrons staid
In their silk and flower'd brocade,
Prim and tall, with soft brows knitted,
Silken aprons, and hands mitted ;
Haggard women, dark of face,
Of the old lost Indian race ;
Maidens happy-eyed and fair,
With bright ribbons in their hair,
Trip along, with eyes cast down,
Thro' the streets of Drowsietown.

Drowsy in the summer day
In the meeting-house sit they;
'Mid the high-back'd pews they doze,
Like bright garden-flowers in rows;
And old Parson Pendon, big
In his gown and silver'd wig,
Drones above in periods fine
Sermons like old flavour'd wine—
Crusted well with keeping long
In the darkness, and not strong.
O! so drowsily he drones
In his rich and sleepy tones,
While the great door, swinging wide,
Shows the bright green street outside,
And the shadows as they pass
On the golden sunlit grass.
Then the mellow organ blows,
And the sleepy music flows,
And the folks their voices raise
In old unctuous hymns of praise,

Fit to reach some ancient god
Half asleep with drowsy nod.
Deep and lazy, clear and low,
Doth the oily organ grow!
Then with sudden golden cease
Comes a silence and a peace;
Then a murmur, all alive,
As of bees within a hive;
And they swarm with quiet feet
Out into the sunny street;
There, at hitching-post and gate
Do the steeds and waggons wait.
Drawn in groups, the gossips talk,
Shaking hands before they walk;
Maids and lovers steal away,
Smiling hand in hand, to stray
By the river, and to say
Drowsy love in the old way—
Till the sleepy sun shines down
On the roofs of Drowsietown.

In the great marsh, far beyond
Street and building, lies the Pond,
Gleaming like a silver shield
In the midst of wood and field ;
There on sombre days you see
Anglers old in reverie,
Fishing feebly morn to night
For the pickerel so bright.
From the woods of beech and fir,
Dull blows of the woodcutter
Faintly sound ; and haply, too,
Comes the cat-owl's wild " tuhoo ! "
Drown'd by distance, dull and deep,
Like a dark sound heard in sleep ;—
And a cock may answer, down
In the depths of Drowsietown.

Such is Drowsietown—but nay !
Was, not *is*, my song should say—
Such *was* summer long ago

In this town so sleepy and slow.
Change has come: thro' wood and dale
Runs the demon of the rail,
And the Drowsietown of yore
Is not drowsy any more!

O so drowsy!   In the haze
Of those long dead summer days,
Underneath the still blue sky
I can see the hamlet lie—
Like a river in a dream
Flows the little nut-brown stream;
Yet not many a mile away
Flashes foam and sprinkles spray,
Close at hand the green marsh flows
Into brackish pools and sloughs,
And with storm-wave fierce and frantic
Roars the wrath of the Atlantic.

Waken Drowsietown?—The Sea?
Break its doze and reverie?

Nay, for if it hears at all
Those unresting waters call,
They are far enough, I guess,
Just to soothe and not distress.
When the wild nor'wester breaks,
And the sullen thunder shakes,
For a space the Town in fear,
Dripping wet with marsh and mere,
Quakes and wonders, and is found
With its ear against the ground
Listening to the sullen war
Of the flashing sea afar!
But the moment all is done
On its tear-drops gleams the sun,
Each rude murmur dies; and lo!
In a sleepy sunny glow,
'Mid the moist rays slanting down,
Once more dozes Drowsietown.

As the place is, drowsy-eyed
Are the folks that there abide;

Strong, phlegmatic, calm, revealing
No wild fantasies of feeling;
Loving sunshine; on the soil
Basking in a drowsy toil.
Mild and mellow, calm and clear,
Flows their life from year to year—
Each fulfils his drowsy labour,
Each the picture of his neighbour,
Each exactly, rich or poor,
What his father was before—
O so drowsy! In a gleam,
Far too steady to be Dream,
Flows their slow humanity
Winding, stealing, to the Sea.

Sea? What Sea? The Waters vast,
Whither all life flows at last,
Where all individual motion
Lost in one imperious ocean
Fades, as yonder river doth
In the great Sea at its mouth.

Ah! the mighty wondrous Deep,
'Tis so near;—yet half asleep,
Deaf to all its busy hum,
These calm people go and come;—
Quite forgetting it is nigh,
Save when hurricanes go by
With a ghostly wail o'erhead
Shrieking shrill—"Bury your dead!"
For a moment, wild-eyed, caught
In a sudden gust of thought,
Panting, praying, wild of face,
Stand the people of the place;
But, directly all is done,
They are smiling in the sun—
Drowsy, yet busy as good bees
Working in a sunny ease,
To and fro, and up and down,
Move the folks of Drowsietown.

II

AFTER MEETING.

DEACON JONES.

WELL, winter's over altogether;
  The loon's come back to Purley Pond;
It's all green grass and pleasant weather
  Up on the marsh and the woods beyond.
It's God Almighty's meaning clear
To give us farmers a prosperous year;
Tho' many a sinner that I could mention
  Is driving his ploughshare nowadays
Clean in the teeth of the Lord's intention,
  And spiling the land he ought to raise.

DEACON HOLMES.

I've drained the marsh by Simpson's building,
  Cleared out the rushes, and flag, and weed,
The ground's all juicy, and looks like yielding,
  And I'm puttin' it down in pip-corn seed.
How's Father Abel? Comin' round?
  Glad the rheumatics have left him now.

DEACON JONES.

Summer's *his* med'cine; he'll soon be sound,
  And spry as a squirrel on a bough.

BIRD CHORUS.

  Chickadee! chickadee!
  Green leaves on every tree!
  Over field, over foam,
  All the birds are coming home.
  Honk! honk! sailing low,
  Cried the gray goose long ago.
  Weet! weet! in the light
  Flutes the phœbe-bird so bright.

Chewink, veery, thrush o' the wood,
  Silver treble raise together;
All around their dainty food
  Ripens with the ripening weather.
Hear, O hear!
In the great elm by the mere
Whip-poor-will is crying clear.

MOTHER ABNER.

And so it is! And so the news is true!
And your Eureka has returned to you;
I saw him in the church, and took a stare.
A Hart, aye every inch, the tallest there.
You'll hold the farm-land now, and keep things
    clear;
You wanted jest a man—Eureka's here.

WIDOW HART.

Well, I don't know. Eureka ain't no hand
At raising crops or looking after land;

It's been a bitter trial to me, neighbour,

To see his wandering ways and hate o' labour.

He's been abroad too much to care jest now

For white men's ways, and following the plough.

MOTHER ABNER.

He's a fine figure and a handsome face ;

There ain't his ekal this day in the place.

And if he'd take a wife and settle down,

There's many a wench would jump in Drowsietown.

Ah! that's the only way to tie your son,

And now he's got the farm 'tis easy done;

There's Jez'bel Jones, and there's Euphemia Clem,

And Sarah Snowe,—they're all good matches,
them.

And there's—why, there he goes, right down
the flat,

Looks almost furrin' in that queer straw hat ;

And who's that with him in the flower'd chintz
dress ?

Why, Phœbe Anna Cattison, I guess!
That little mite! How tiny and how prim
Trips little Phœbe by the side of him!
And when she looks up in his face, tehee!
It's like a chipmunk looking up a tree!

THE RIVER SINGS.

O willow loose lightly
  Your soft long hair!
I'll brush it brightly
  With tender care;
And past you flowing
  I'll softly uphold
Great lilies blowing
  With hearts of gold.
For spring is beaming,
  The wind's in the south,
And the musk-rat's swimming,
  A twig in its mouth,

I

To build its nest
Where it loves it best,
In the great dark nook
By the bed o' my brook.
It's spring, bright spring,
And blue-birds sing !
And the fern is pearly
  All day long,
And the lark rises early
  To sing a song.
The grass shoots up like fingers of fire,
And the flowers awake to a dim desire,
So willow, willow, shake down, shake down
  Your locks so silvern and long and slight;
For lovers are coming from Drowsietown,
  And thou and I must be merry and bright !

PHŒBE ANNA.

This is the first fine day this year :
The grass is dry and the sky is clear ;
The sun's out shining ; up to the farm

It looks like summer; so bright and warm.
There's apple blooms on the boughs already,
   Long as your finger the corn-blades shoot,
And father thinks, if the sun keeps steady,
   'Twill be a wonderful fall for fruit.
How do you like being here at home again ?
Reckon you'd rather pack up and roam again !

EUREKA.

I'm sick o' roaming, I hate strange places;
   I've slep' too long in the woods and brakes;
It's pleasure seeing white folks' faces
   After the b'ars, and the birds, and the snakes.
This yer life is civilisation,
T'other's a heathen dissipation !
One likes to die where his father before him
Died, with the same sky shinin' o'er him.
I've been a wastrel and that's the truth,
   Earning nought but a sneer and a frown;
I've wasted the precious days o' youth,
   Instead of stopping and settling down.

PHŒBE ANNA.

But now the farm is your own to dwell in,
  You'll ne'er go back to the wilderness?

EUREKA.

Waal! that's a question! There's no tellin';
  I ain't my own master quite, I guess.
Think I shall *have* to go some day,
And fix some business far away.
I—there's your mother beckonin' yonder,
  Looks kind o' huffish, you'd better run;
(Alone, sotto voce) That girl's a sort of a shinin'
    wonder,
  The prettiest pout beneath the sun.

BIRD CHORUS.

  Chickadee! chickadee!
  Green leaves on every tree;
  Winter goes, spring is here;
  Little mate, we loved last year.

Cheewink, veery, robin red,
   Shall we take another bride?
We have plighted, we are wed.
   Here we gather happy-eyed.
Little bride, little mate,
Shall I leave you desolate?
Men change; shall we change too?
Men change; but we are true.
If I cease to love thee best,
May a black boy take my nest.

EUREKA.

Soothin' it is, after so many a year,
To hear the Sabbath bells a-ringing clear,
The air so cool and soft, the sky so blue,
The place so peaceful and so well-to-do. . . .
Wonder what *she* is doing this same day?
Thinkin' o' me in her wild Injin way,
Listenin' and waitin', dreaming every minute
The door will open, and this child step in it.

Poor gal! I seem to feel her eyes so bright
A-followin' me about, morn, noon, and night!
Sometimes they make me start and thrill right
    thro'—
She was a splendid figure, and that's true!
Not jest like Christian women, fair and white,
A heap more startlin' and a deal more bright;
And as for looks, why many would prefer
That Phœbe Ann, or some white gal like her!
Don't know! *I*'ve got no call to judge; but see!
The little white wench is so spry and free!
And tho' she's but a mite, small as a mouse,
She'd look uncommon pretty in a house.
No business, tho', of mine—I've made my bed,
And I must lie in it, as I have said.
Ye . . . s, I'll go back—and stay—or bring her
    here,
But there's no call to hurry yet, that's clear.
She'll fret and be impatient for a while,
And go on in the wild mad Injin style;

But she can't know, for a clear heathen's sake,

The sort o' sacrifice I'm fix'd to make.

Some wouldn't do it; Parson there would say

It's downright throwing next world's chance

    away;

But I've made up my mind—it's fix'd at present;

And—there, let's try to think of something

    pleasant!

THE CAT-OWL.

Boohoo! boohoo!

White man is not true;

I have seen such wicked ways

That I hide me all the days,

And come from my hole so deep

When the white man lies asleep.

A misanthrope am I,

    And, tho' the skies are blue,

I utter my warning cry—

    Boohoo!

Boohoo! boohoo! boohoo!

THE LOON.

(Chuckling to himself on the pond.)

Ha! ha! ha! back again,
Thro' the frost and fog and rain;
Winter's over now, that's plain.
Ha! ha! ha! back again!
And I laugh and scream,
    For I love so well
The bright, bright bream,
    And the pickerel!
And soft is my breast,
    And my bill is keen,
And I'll build my nest
    'Mid the sedge unseen.

I've travell'd—I've fish'd in the sunny south,
In the mighty mere, at the harbour mouth;
I've seen fair countries, all golden and gay;
    I've seen bright pictures that beat all wishing;
I've found fine colours afar away—
    But give me Purley Pond, for fishing;

Of all the ponds, north, south, east, west,
This is the pond I love the best;
For all is quiet, and few folk peep,
  Save some of the innocent angling people;
And I like on Sundays, half asleep,
All alone on the pool so deep,
  To rock and hear the bells from the steeple.
And I laugh so clear that all may hear
The loon is back, and summer is near.
Ha! ha! ha! so merry and plain
I laugh with joy to be home again.

    (*A shower passes over; all things sing.*)

  The swift is wheeling and gleaming,
    The brook is brown in its bed,
  Rain from the cloud is streaming,
    And the Bow bends overhead.
The charm of the winter is broken! the last of
  the spell is said!

The eel in the pond is quick'ning,
　　The grayling leaps in the stream—
What if the clouds are thick'ning?
　　See how the meadows gleam!
The spell of the winter is shaken; the world
　　awakes from a dream!

The fir puts out green fingers,
　　The pear-tree softly blows,
The rose in her dark bower lingers,
　　But her curtains will soon unclose,
The lilac will shake her ringlets over the blush
　　of the rose.

The swift is wheeling and gleaming,
　　The woods are beginning to ring,
Rain from the cloud is streaming;—
　　There, where the Bow doth cling,
Summer is smiling afar off, over the shoulder of
　　Spring!

III

PHŒBE ANNA.

DIMPLED, dainty, one-and-twenty,
　Rosy-faced and round of limb,
Warm'd with mother-wit in plenty,
　Prudent, modest, spry yet prim,
Lily-handed, tiny-footed,
　With an ankle clean and neat,
Neatly gloved and trimly booted,
　Looking nice and smelling sweet!
Self-possess'd, subduing beauty
To a sober sense of duty,
Chaste as Dian, plump as Hebe,
Such I guess was little Phœbe.

O how different a creature
  From that other wondrous woman!
Not a feeling, not a feature,
  Had these two fair flowers in common.
One was tall and moulded finely,
  Large of limb, and grand of gaze,
Rich with incense, and divinely
  Throbbing into passionate rays,—
Lustrous-eyed and luscious-bosom'd,
  Beautiful, and richly rare,
As a passion-flower full blossom'd,
  Born to Love and Love's despair.
Such was Red Rose; and the other?
  Tiny, prudish, if you please,
Meant to be a happy mother,
  With a bunch of huswife's keys.
Prudent, not to be deluded,
Happy-eyed and sober-mooded,
Dainty, mild, yet self-reliant,
  She, as I'm a worthy singer,

Wound our vacillating giant
　　Round her little dimpled finger.

Bit by bit, a bashful wooer,
　　Fascinated unaware,
Did Eureka draw unto her,
　　Tame as any dancing bear.
Not a finger did she stir,
Yet he glow'd and gazed at her!
Not a loving look she gave,
Yet he watch'd her like a slave!
He, who had been used to having
Pleasures past all human craving,
Who had idly sat and taken
Showers of kisses on him shaken,
Who had fairly tired of passion
Ever felt in passive fashion,
Now stood blushing like a baby
In the careless eyes of Phœbe!

Fare ye well, O scenes of glory,
　　One bright sheet of golden sheen!

Love, the spirit of my story,
  Wakens in a different scene.
Down the lanes, so tall and leafy,
  Falls Eureka's loving feet,
Following Phœbe's, but in chief he
  In the kitchen loves to sit,—
Loves to watch her, tripping ruddy
  In the rosy firelight glow,
Loves to watch, in a brown study,
  The warm figure come and go.

Half indifferent unto him,
Far too wise to coax and woo him,
Ill-disposed to waste affection,
Full of modest circumspection,
Quite the bright superior being,
Tho' so tiny to the seeing,
With a mind which penetrated,
  In a sly and rosy mirth,

Thro' the face, and estimated
   Grain by grain the spirit's worth,
Phœbe Anna, unenraptured,
Led the creature she had captured.

What is Love ? A shooting star,
Flying, flashing, lost afar.
What is Man ? A fretful boy,
Ever seeking some new toy.
What is Memory ? Alas !
'Tis a strange magician's glass,
Where you pictures bright may mark
If you hold it *in the dark*.
Thrust it out into the sun,
All the picturing is done,
And the magic dies away
In the golden glow of day !

Coming back to civilisation,
   Petted, fêted, shone on daily,

Was a novel dissipation,
   And Eureka revell'd gaily.
Friendly faces flash'd around him,
   Church-bells tinkled in his ear,
Cosy cronies sought and found him,
   Drowsietown look'd bright and clear.
Parson Pendon and his lady
   (Respectability embodied)
Welcom'd the stray sheep already,
   Matrons smiled, and deacons nodded.
Uncle Pete had left him lately
   Malden Farm and all its store,
And he found himself prized greatly
   As a worthy bachelor.
All his roaming days seem'd over!
   Like a beast without a load,
Grazing in the golden clover,
   In the village he abode!
And he loved the tilth and tillage,
All the bustle of the village—

Loved the reaping and the sowing,
  Loved the music of the mill,
Loved to see the mowers mowing,
And the golden grasses growing,
  Breast-deep, near the river still.
Civilisation altogether
  Seem'd exactly to his notion!
Life was like good harvest weather,
  Faintly flavoured with devotion.
Ruefully he cogitated,
  With the peaceful spire in sight :—
" Waal, I guess the thing was fated,
  And it's hard to set it right.
Seems a dream, too! now, I wonder
  If it seems a dream to *her* !
After that first parting stunn'd her,
  For a time she'd make a stir;
P'raps, tho', when the shock was over,
Other sentiments might move her!
First she'd cry, next, she'd grow fretful,

K

Thirdly, riled, and then forgetful.
After all that's done and said,
  Injin blood is Injin ever!
I'm a white skin, she's a red;
  Providence just made us sever.
Parson says that sort of thing
Isn't moral marrying!
Tho' the simple creature yonder
  Had no better education—
Ignorance jest made her fonder,
  And *I* yielded to temptation.
Here's the question : I've been sinning—
Wrong, clean wrong, from the beginning;
Can I make my blunder better
  By repeating it again?
When mere Nature, if I let her,
  Soon can cure the creature's pain;
She'll forget me fast enough—
  And she's no religious feeling;
Injin hearts are always tough,

And their wounds are quick of healing.
Heigho!"—here he sighed; then seeing
   Phœbe Ann trip by in laughter,
Brightening up, the bother'd being
   Shook off care, and trotted after!

Had this final complication
   Not been added to the rest;
Had not Fate with new temptation
   Drugg'd the conscience of his breast,
Possibly his better nature
   Might have triumph'd o'er the treason;
But the passions of the creature
   Rose in league with his false reason;
On the side of civilisation
   Rose the pretty Civilisee:
In a flush of new sensation,
   Conscience died, and Shame did flee.
That bright picture, many-colour'd,
Nature had flash'd before the dullard;

That wild ecstasy and rapture
She had tamed unto his capture—
That grand form, intensely burning
To a lightning-flash of yearning—
That fair face transfigur'd brightly
Into starry rapture nightly—
Those large limbs of living lustre,
 Moving with a flower-like grace—
Those great joys which hung in cluster,
 Like ripe fruit in a green place—
All had faded from his vision,
 And instead, before his sight,
Tript the pretty-faced precisian,
 Deep and dimpled, warm and white!

In her very style of looking
There was cognisance of cooking!
From her very dress were peeping
Indications of housekeeping!

You might gather in a minute,
  As she lightly passed you by,
She could (with her whole heart in it!)
  Nurse a babe or make a pie.
Yet her manner and expression
  Shook the foolish giant's nerve,
With their quiet self-possession
  And their infinite reserve.

In his former time the wooing
Had been all the *female's* doing;
He had waited while the other
Did his soul with raptures smother!
But 'twas quite another matter,
  Here in civilisation's school!
And his heart went pitter-patter,
  And he trembled like a fool.
Thro' the church the road lay to her;—
  That was written on her face,
Lawfully the man must woo her
  In the manner of her race.

So by slow degrees he enter'd,

Courtship's Maze so mystic-centred!

Round and round the pathways wander'd,

Made his blunders, puzzled, ponder'd;

Laugh'd at, laughing, scorn'd, imploring,

Mad, enraged, distraught, adoring;

This way, that way, turning, twisting;

Yielding oft, and oft resisting:

Gasping while the voice of Cupid

Madden'd him with "Hither, stupid!"

Seeking ever for the middle

Of the green and golden riddle—

Oft, just as he cried, "I've got it!"

Finding *culs de sac*, and not it!

Till at last his blunders ended

On a summer morning splendid,

When with vision glad and hazy,

   Seeing Phœbe blushing falter,

In the centre of the Maze, he

   Found himself before—an Altar!

IV

NUPTIAL SONG.

Where were they wedded ?   In the holy house
  Built up by busy fingers ?
All Drowsietown was quiet as a mouse
  To hear the village singers.

Who was the Priest ?   'Twas Parson Pendon,
    dress'd
  In surplice to the knuckles,
Wig powder'd, snowy cambric on his breast,
  Silk stockings, pumps, and buckles.

What was the service ?   'Twas the solemn, stale,
  Old-fashion'd, English measure :
" Wilt thou this woman take ? and thou this
    male ? "
  " I will "—" I will "—with pleasure.

Who saw it done ?   The countless rustic eyes
  Of folk around them thronging.
Who shared the joy ?   The matrons with soft
    sighs,
  The girls with bright looks longing.

Who was the bride ?   Sweet Phœbe, dress'd in
    clothes
  As white as she who wore 'em,
Sweet-scented, self-possess'd,—one bright White
    Rose
  Of virtue and decorum.

Her consecration ?   Peaceful self-control,
  And modest circumspection—
The sweet old service softening her soul
  To formulised affection.

Surveying with calm eyes the long, straight road
  Of matrimonial being,
She wore her wedding clothes, trusting in God,
  Domestic, and far-seeing.

With steady little hand she sign'd her name,
  Nor trembled at the venture.
What did the Bridegroom? Blush'd with sheepish
    shame,
  Endorsing the indenture.

O Hymen, Hymen! In the church so calm
  Began the old sweet story,
The parson smiled, the summer fields breathed
    balm,
  The crops were in their glory.

Out from the portal came the wedding crew,
  All smiling, palpitating ;—
And there was Jacob with the cart, bran new,
  And the white pony, waiting.

The girls waved handkerchiefs, the village boys
  Shouted, around them rushing,
And off they trotted thro' the light and noise,
  She calm, the giant blushing.

Down the green road, along by glade and grove,
  They jog, with rein-bells jingling,
The orchards pink all round, the sun above,
  She cold, Eureka tingling.

And round her waist his arm becomes entwined,
  But still her ways are coolish—
"There's old Dame Dartle looking! Don't now! Mind
  The pony! Guess you're foolish!"

Who rang the bells? The ringers with a will
  Set them in soft vibration.
Hark! loud and clear, there chimes o'er vale and hill
  The nuptial jubilation.

Part IV.

THE GREAT SNOW.

I

THE GREAT SNOW.

'TWAS the year of the Great Snow.

First the East began to blow
Chill and shrill for many days,
On the wild wet woodland ways.
Then the North, with crimson cheeks,
Blew upon the pond for weeks,
Chill'd the water thro' and thro',
Till the first thin ice-crust grew
Blue and filmy; then at last
All the pond was frosted fast,
Prison'd, smother'd, fetter'd tight,
Let it struggle as it might.

And the first Snow drifted down
On the roofs of Drowsietown.

First the vanguard of the Snow;
Falling flakes, whirling slow,
Drifting darkness, troubled dream;
Then a motion and a gleam;
Sprinkling with a carpet white
   Orchards, swamps, and woodland ways,
Thus the first Snow took its flight,
   And there was a hush for days.

Mid that hush the Spectre dim,
Faint of breath and thin of limb,
HOAR-FROST, like a maiden's ghost,
Nightly o'er the marshes crost
In the moonlight: where she flew,
   At the touch of her chill dress
Cobwebs of the glimmering dew
   Froze to silvern loveliness.

All the night, in the dim light,
Quietly she took her flight;
Thro' the streets she crept, and stayed
In each silent window shade,
With her finger moist as rain
Drawing flowers upon the pane;—
On the phantom flowers so drawn
   With her frozen breath breath'd she;
And each window-pane at dawn
   Turn'd to crystal tracery!

Then the Phantom Fog came forth,
Following slowly from the North;
Wheezing, coughing, blown, and damp,
He sat sullen in the swamp,
Scowling with a blood-shot eye
As the canvas-backs went by;
Till the North Wind with a shout,
Thrust his pole and poked him out;

And the Phantom with a scowl,
  Black'ning night and dark'ning day,
Hooted after by the owl,
  Lamely halted on his way.

Now in flocks that ever increase
Honk the armies of the geese,
'Gainst a sky of crimson red
Silhouetted overhead.
After them in a dark mass,
Sleet and hail hiss as they pass,
Rattling on the frozen lea
With their shrill artillery.
Then a silence : then comes on
Frost, the steel-bright Skeleton !
Silent in the night he steals,
With wolves howling at his heels,
Seeing to the locks and keys
On the ponds and on the leas.
Touching with his tingling wand
Trees and shrubs on every hand,

Till they change, transform'd to sight,
Into dwarfs and druids white,—
Icicle-bearded, frosty-shrouded
Underneath his mantle clouded ;
And on many of their shoulders,
Chill, indifferent to beholders,
Sits the barr'd owl in a heap,
Ruffled, dumb, and fast asleep.
There the legions of the trees
Gather ghost-like round his knees ;
While in cloudy cloak and hood,
Cold he creeps to the great wood :—
Lying there in a half-doze,
While on finger-tips and toes
Squirrels turn their wheels, and jays
Flutter in a wild amaze,
And the foxes, lean and foul,
Look out of their holes and growl.
There he waiteth, breathing cold
On the white and silent wold.

L

In a silence sat the Thing,
Looking north, and listening!
And the farmers drave their teams
Past the woods and by the streams,
Crying as they met together,
With chill noses, " *Frosty weather !* "
And along the iron ways
Tinkle, tinkle, went the sleighs.
And the wood-chopper did hie,
Leather stockings to the thigh,
Crouching on the snow that strew'd
Every corner of the wood.
Still Frost waited, very still;
Then he whistled, loud and shrill;
Then he pointed north, and lo!
The main Army of the Snow.

Black as Erebus afar,
Blotting sun, and moon, and star,

Drifting, in confusion driven,
Screaming, straggling, rent and riven,
Whirling, wailing, blown afar
In an awful wind of War,
Dragging drifts of dead beneath,
  With a melancholy groan,
While the fierce Frost set his teeth,
  Rose erect, and waved them on!

All day long the legions passed
On an ever-gathering blast;
In an ever-gathering night,
Fast they eddied on their flight.
With a tramping and a roar,
Like the waves on a wild shore;
With a motion and a gleam,
Whirling, driven in a dream;
On they drave in drifts of white,
Burying Drowsietown from sight,

Covering ponds, and woods and roads,
Shrouding trees and men's abodes;
While the great Pond loaded deep,
Turning over in its sleep,
Groaned;—but when night came, forsooth,
　Grew the tramp unto a thunder;
Wind met wind with wail uncouth,
Frost and Storm fought nail and tooth,
　Shrieking, and the roofs rock'd under.
Scared out of its sleep that night,
Drowsietown awoke in fright;
Chimney-pots above it flying,
　Windows crashing to the ground,
Snow-flakes blinding, multiplying,
　Snow-drift whirling round and round;
While, whene'er the strife seemed dying,
The great North-wind, shrilly crying,
　Clash'd his shield in battle-sound!

Multitudinous and vast,
Legions after legions passed.

Still the air behind was drear
With new legions coming near ;
Still they waver'd, wander'd on,
Glimmer'd, trembled, and were gone.
While the drift grew deeper, deeper,
  On the roofs and at the doors,
While the wind awoke each sleeper
  With its melancholy roars.
Once the Moon looked out, and lo !
Blind against her face the Snow
Like a wild white grave-cloth lay,
Till she shuddering crept away.
Then thro' darkness like the grave,
On and on the legions drave.

When the dawn came, Drowsietown
  Smother'd in the snow-drift lay.
Still the swarms were drifting down
  In a dark and dreadful day.

On the blinds the whole day long
　Thro' the red light shadows flitted.
At the inn in a great throng
　Gossips gather'd drowsy-witted.
All around on the white lea
Farm-lamps twinkled drearily ;
Not a road was now revealed,
　Drift, deep drift, at every door ;
Field was mingled up with field,
　Stream and pond were smother'd o'er,
Trees and fences fled from sight
In the deep wan waste of white.

Many a night, many a day,
Pass'd the wonderful array,
Sometimes in confusion driven,
By the dreadful winds of heaven ;
Sometimes gently wavering by
With a gleam and smothered sigh,

While the lean Frost still did stand
Pointing with his skinny hand
Northward, with the shrubs and trees
Buried deep below his knees.
Still the Snow passed; deeper down
In the snow sank Drowsietown.
Not a bird stayed, big or small,
Not a team could stir at all.
Round the cottage window-frame
Barking foxes nightly came,
Scowling in a spectral ring
At the ghostly glimmering.
Old Abe Sinker at the Inn
Heap'd his fire up with a grin,
For the great room, warm and bright,
Never emptied morn or night.
Old folks shiver'd with their bones
Full of pains and cold as stones.
Nought was doing, nought was done,
From the rise to set of sun.

Yawning in the ale-house heat,
Shivering in the snowy street,
Like dream-shadows, up and down,
   With their footprints black below,
Moved the folk of Drowsietown,
   In the Year of the Great Snow!

II

THE WANDERER.

SNOWING and blowing, roaring and rattle,
Frost, snow, and wind are all busy at battle!
O what a quaking, and shaking, and calling,
Whitely, so whitely, the snow still is falling;
Stone-dead the earth is, shrouded all over,
White, stiff, and hard is the snow-sheet above her,
Deep, deep the drift is; and tho' it is snowing,
Blacker, yet blacker, the heavens are growing.
Oh, what a night! gather nearer the fire!
Pile the warm pine-logs higher and higher;
Shut the black storm out, close tight the
    shutters,
Hark! how without there it moans and it
    mutters,

Tearing with teeth, claws, and fingers tre-
    mendous,
Roof, wall, and gable !—now Angels defend us !
There was a roar !—how it crashes and darkens !
No wonder that Phœbe stops, trembles, and
    hearkens.

For black as the skies are, tho' hueless and
    ghastly,
Stretches the wold, 'mid the snow falling fastly,
Here in the homestead by Phœbe made cosy,
All is so pleasant, so ruddy, and rosy.
All by herself in the tile-paven kitchen,
In white huswife's gown, and in apron bewitching,
Flits little Phœbe, so busily making
Corn bread and rye bread for Saturday's baking.
See ! in the firelight that round her is gleaming,
How she is glowing, and glancing, and beaming,
While all around her, in sheer perspiration
Of an ecstatic and warm admiration,

Plates, cups, and dishes, delightedly glowing,

Watch her sweet shade as 'tis coming and going,

Catch her bright image as lightly she passes,

Shine it about in plates, dishes, and glasses!

Often in wonder all trembling and quaking,

To feel how the homestead is swaying and shaking,

All in a clatter they cry out together,

"The roof will be off in a minute!   What
  weather!"

. . . . A face in the darkness, a foot on the Snow,

Is it there? Dost thou hear? Doth it come?
  Doth it go?

Hush! only the gusts as they gather and grow.

O Phœbe is busy!—with little flour'd fingers,

Like rosebuds in snow, o'er her labour she
  lingers;

And oft when the tumult is loudest she listens,

Her eyes are intent, and her pretty face glistens

So warm in the firelight.   Despite the storm's
    crying,

Sound, sound in their slumbers the farm-maids
    are lying ;

The clock with its round face perspiring and
    blinking,

Is pointing to bed-time, and sleepily winking.

The sheep-dog lies basking, the grey cat is
    purring,

Only the tempest is crying and stirring.

The minutes creep on, and the wind still is busy,

And Phœbe still hearkens, perplex'd, and un-
    easy.

. . . . A face in the wold where the snowdrift
    lies low.

A footfall by night ?—or the winds as they blow ?

O hush ! it comes nearer, a foot on the Snow.

Phœbe's fond heart is beginning to flutter,

She hearks for a footfall, a tap on the shutter;

She lists for a voice while the storm gathers
    shriller,

The drift's at the door, and the frost groweth
    chiller.

She looks at the clock, and she starteth back
    sighing,

While the cuckoo leaps out from his hole in it,
    crying

His name ten times over; past ten, little singer!

"O what keeps Eureka? and where can he
    linger?"

The snow is so deep, and the ways are so dire,

She thinks; and a footfall comes nigher and
    nigher.

. . . . A face in the darkness, a face full of woe,

A face and a footfall—they come and they go,

Still nearer and nearer—a foot on the Snow!

Eureka's abroad in the town,—but 'tis later

Than Drowsietown's bed-time. Still greater
    and greater

The fears of poor Phœbe each moment are
    growing;

And sadder and paler her features are glowing.

She steps to the door—lifts the latch—with wild
    scolding

The door is dashed open, and torn from her
    holding,

While shivering she peers on the blackness,
    vibrating

With a trouble of whiteness within it pulsating !

The wind piles the drift at the threshold before her,

The snow swarms upon her, around her, and o'er
    her,

But melts on the warmth of her face and her
    hands.

A moment in trouble she hearkens and
    stands.

All black and all still, save the storm's wild
    tabor !

And she closes the door, and comes back to her
    labour.

In vain—she grows paler—her heart sinks within
    her,

The cuckoo bursts out in a flutter (the sinner),

And chimes the half-hour—she sits now await-
    ing,

Her heart forbodes evil, her mind still debating;

The drift is so deep—could a false step within it

Have led to his grave in one terrible minute ?

Could his foot have gone wand'ring away in the
    wold there,

While frozen and feeble he sank in the cold
    there ?

'Tis his foot ! . . . Nay, not yet ! . . . There he's
    tapping, to summon

His wife to the door ! Nay, indeed, little
    woman !

'Tis his foot at the door!—and he listens to hear
　　her!

Nay, not yet; yet a footfall there *is*, coming
　　nearer.

A face in the darkness, a foot on the Snow,

Nearer it comes to the warm window-glow;

O hush! thro' the wind, a foot-fall on the Snow.

Now heark, Phœbe, heark!—But she hearks not;
　　for dreaming,

Her soft eyes are fixed on the fire's rosy gleam-
　　ing;

Hands crossed on her knees she rocks to and fro;

O heark! Phœbe, heark! 'tis a foot on the Snow.

O heark! Phœbe, heark! and flit over the floor,

'Tis a foot on the snow! 'tis a tap at the door!

Low, faint as hail tapping. . . Upstarting, she
　　hearkens.

It ceases. The firelight sinks low, the room
　　darkens.

She listens again. All is still. The wind
  blowing,
The thrill of the tempest, the sound of the snowing.
Hush again! something taps—a low murmur is
  heard.
"Come in," Phœbe cries; but the latch is not
  stirred.

Her heart's failing fast; superstitious and mute
She stands and she trembles, and stirs not a foot.
She hears a low breathing, a moaning, a knock,
Between the wind's cry and the tick of the clock:
Tap! tap! .. with an effort she shakes off her fear,
Makes one step to the door; again pauses to
  hear.
The latch stirs; in terror and desperate haste
She opens the door, shrinking back pallid-faced,
And sees at the porch, with a thrill of affright,
'Mid the gleaming of snow and the darkness of
  night,

M

A shape like a Woman's, a tremulous form

White with the snow-flakes and bent with the
    storm!

Great eyes looking out through a black tatter'd
    hood,

With a gleam of wild sorrow that thrills through
    the blood,

A hand that outreaches, a voice sadly strung,

That speaks to her soul in some mystical tongue!

The face in the darkness, the foot on the Snow,

They have come, they are here, with their weal
    and their woe:

O long was the journey! the wayfarer slow!

Now Phœbe hath courage, for plainly the being

She looks on is mortal, though wild to the
    seeing—

Tall, spectral, and strange, yet in sorrow so
    human—

And the eyes, though so wild, are the eyes of a
    woman.

Her face is all hid; but her brow and her hands,

And the quaint ancient cloak that she wears as
    she stands,

Are those of the red race who still wander
    scatter'd—

The gipsies of white towns, dishonour'd, drink-
    shatter'd.

And strange, too, she seems by her tongue; yet
    her words are

As liquid and soft as the notes of a bird are.

All this in a moment sees Phœbe; then lo!

She sees the shape staggering in from the
    snow,

Revealing, as in to the fire-gleam she goes,

A face wild with famine, and haggard with
    woes,

For her hood falls away, and her head glimmers
  bare,

And loosen'd around falls her dank dripping
  hair,

And her eyes gleam like death—she would fall
  to the earth,

But the soft little hands of kind Phœbe reach
  forth,

And lead her, half swooning, half conscious,
  until

She sinks in a chair by the fire and is still ;

Still, death-like,—while Phœbe kneels down by
  her chair,

And chafes her chill hands with a motherly care.

The face is upon her, it gleams in the glow,

She hears a voice warning, still dreadful and
  low,

Far back lies the footprint, a track in the Snow.

The woman was ghost-like, yet wondrously fair

Through the gray cloud of famine, the dews of
   despair,

Her face hunger'd forth—'twas a red woman's face,

Without the sunk eyeball, the taint of the race ;

With strange gentle lines round the mouth of
   her, cast

By moments of being too blissful to last.

Her cloak fallen wide, as she sat there distraught,

Revealed a strange garment with figures en-
   wrought

In silk and old beads—it had once been most
   bright—

But frayed with long wearing by day and by
   night.

Mocassins she wore, and they, too, had been
   gay,

But now they were ragged and rent by the
   way ;

And bare to the cold was one foot, soft and red,
And frozen felt both, and one trickled and bled.

The face of the stranger, 'tis worn with its woe,
It comes to thee, Phœbe, but when shall it go?
Far back go the footprints; see! black in the
 Snow.

But look! what is that? lo! it lies on her breast,
A small living creature, an infant at rest!
So tiny, so shrivell'd, a mite of red clay,
Warm, mummied, and wrapt in the Indian way.
It opens its eyes, and it shrivels red cheeks;
It thrusts out its hand to the face, and it speaks
With a cry to the heart of the mother; and lo!
She stirs from her swoon, and her famish'd
 cheeks glow,
She rolls her wild eyes at the cry of distress,
And her weak hands instinctively open her dress

That the babe may be fed ; and the touch of the
    child

When it comes to her bosom, warm, milky, and
    mild,

Seems blissful—she smiles—O, so faintly !—is
    blest

To feel its lips draw at the poor weary breast.

She closes her eyes, she is soothed, and her form

Within the great firelight grows happy and
    warm.

She hears not the wind, and she seems in a
    dream,

Till her orbs startle open amid the glad gleam ;

Her looks fall on Phœbe, who trembles for pity;

She holds out her hands with a cry of
    entreaty;

Her thoughts flow together—she knows the
    bright place,

She feels the sweet firelight, she sees the kind
    face—

For Phœbe unloosens her poor dripping cloak,

And its damp rises up in the kitchen like
  smoke;

And Phœbe, with tender and matronly grace,

Is wiping the snow and the wet from her face.

She looks, sinks again, speaks with quick bird-
  like cries,

In her own thrilling speech; but her voice
  breaks and dies,

And her tears, through shut eyelids, ooze slowly
  and blindly

On the white little hands that are touching her
  kindly.

A face in the darkness, a face full of woe,

Deep, deep, are the white ways, and bleak the
  winds blow;

O, long was the journey, the wayfarer slow,

O, look! black as death, stretch the prints in
  the Snow.

III

RETROSPECT: THE JOURNEY.

A FOOTPRINT—trace it back.   O God!
The bleeding feet, the weary road.
Fly, Fancy, as the eagle flies,
With beating heart and burning eyes,
Fly on the north-wind's breath of power,
Beat mile by mile, and hour by hour,
Southward, still southward: shouldst thou tire
Rest with the solar sphere of fire,
Then rise again and take thy flight
Across the continent in white,
And track, still track, as thou dost go
This bleeding footprint in the snow!
Fly night by night, or day by day,
Count the long hours, watch the wild way;

Then see, beneath thee sailing swift
The white way melteth, and the drift
Gathers no longer; and instead
Of snow a dreary rain is shed,
On grassy ways, on dreary leas,
And sullen pools that do not freeze.
Now must thy keen eye look more near
To trace the bloody footprint here;
But see! still see! it can be traced
On the wet pastures of the waste;
On! on, still on! still southward sail,
While tall trees shake in the shrill gale,
And great streams gather, and things green
Begin to show thro' the dim sheen.
Here thro' a mighty wood the track
Errs like a silk thread slowly back,
And here birds singing go and come,
Tho' far away the world is dumb.
A river, and the track is lost.
But when the stream is safely cross'd

Again, upon the further brim,
The drop of blood, the footprint dim !
O wingèd thought, o'er half a world
Thou sailest with great wings unfurl'd,
From white to dark, from dark to bright,
From north to south, thou takest flight,
Passing with constant waft of wing
From winter climes to climes of spring,
Swiftly thou goest, and still thy gaze
Follows the footprint thro' wild ways ;
Swiftly thou speedest south—O God !
A thousand leagues of weary road !

A thousand leagues ! O see, the track,
Clear to the soul's eye, wavers back
Dim yet unbroken, linking slow
Winter with spring, sunshine with snow,
The dead leaf with the leaf still blowing,
The frozen stream with the stream flowing ;
Linking and binding silently
Forgetfulness with memory,

Love living with love long at rest,
A burning with a frozen breast,
A Sunbeam Soul all light and seeing
With a mere Beaver of a being.

Turn back, my Spirit, turn and trace
The woman from her starting place,
Whence with fix'd features and feet free
She plunged into the world's great Sea,—
A fair sweet swimmer, strong of limb,
Most confident in God, and *him*,
And found herself by wild winds blown,
In a great waste, alone, alone!

Long with the patience of her race,
Had Red Rose waited for the face
That came not, listen'd for the voice
That made her soul leap and rejoice.
They came not : all was still.   For days,
She like a fawn in the green ways

Wander'd alone; and night by night
She watch'd heaven's eye of liquid light
With eyes as luminous as theirs,
'Mid tremulous sighs and panted prayers.
He came not: all was still: her tread
Grew heavier on the earth, her head
Hung sadder, and her weeping eyes,
Look'd more on earth than on the skies:
Like a dead leaf she droop'd in woe,
Until one day, with a quick throe,
She turn'd to crimson as she wept,
And lo! within her something leapt!

Flesh of her flesh, the blossom broke,
  Blood of her blood, she felt it stir,
Within her life another woke
  With still small eyes, and look'd at her!
And with a strange ecstatic pain,
She breathed, and felt it breathe again.

She seem'd to see it night and day,

Coming along from far away

Down a green path, and with fierce flame

She rush'd to meet it as it came,

But as she rush'd the shape did seem

Suddenly to dissolve in dream,

And daily she stood hungering sore,

Till far off it arose once more.

But as the life within her grew

   A horror took away her breath,

Lest when her cruel kinsmen knew

   Her secret, they should deal her death.

For now the aged Chief, with whom

Her happy life had broke to bloom,

Along the dark deep path had wound

That leads to God's great hunting-ground;

And a young brave of the red band

Was proudly wooing for her hand;—

Not in white fashion fervently,
Not with wild vows and on his knee;
Rather a proud majestic wooer
Who felt his suit an honour to her,
And who his formal presents sent
In calm assumption of consent,
And never dream'd the maid would dare
To turn her tender eyes elsewhere;—
Nor dared she openly disdain
A suit so solemn and so plain;
But with a smile half agonized
She (as we whites say) temporized!

She found two friendly women, who,
Tho' hags in form, were kind and true,
And with their aid, when the hour came,
She bare her child and hid her shame.
As Eve bare Cain, upon a bed
Of balsam and of hemlock, spread
By those kind hands, in the deep woods,
Amid the forest solitudes,

With myriad creatures round her flying,

And every creature multiplying;

In the warm greenwood, hid from sight,

She held her babe to the glad light,

And brighten'd.   As she linger'd there,

She had a dream most sadly fair,

She seem'd upon a river-side,

Gazing across a crystal tide,

And o'er the tide in dying swells

There came a burthen as of bells

Out of a mist; then the mist clear'd,

And on the further bank appear'd

A dim shape fondly beckoning—

Her warrior tall, her heart's white King!

She cried, and woke; the dream was nought;

But ever after her wild thought

Yearn'd with an instinct mad and dumb

To seek him, since he did not come.

She thought, " My warrior beckons me!

He would be here if he were free.

And if I stay my kinsmen wild
Will surely slay me and the child;
But there, with *him* in that fair place,
Where he is chief of his own race,
All will be well; for he is good,
Of milder race and gentler blood;
And tho' I die upon the way
'Twill not be worse than if I stay,
Butcher'd and shamed in all men's sight
When my sad secret comes to light.
'Tis well! this paper in my hand
Will guide my footsteps thro' the land,
And when I strengthen I will fly,
And I will find my lord, or die!"
'Twas thought, 'twas done; at dead of night,
She clasp'd her infant and took flight.

One guide she had—the luminous star,
On the horizon line afar;

For thither oft Eureka's hand
Had pointed, telling her his land
Lay thitherward : gazing thereon,
That night she busied to be gone,
It seem'd a lamp that he had placed
To guide her footsteps o'er the waste.
She gather'd food, then to her back
Attach'd the babe, and took the track,
Waving her hands in wild " adieu "
To those kind women dark of hue,
Who crouching on a dark ascent
Moan'd low, and watch'd her as she went.
There shone the star liquid and clear,
His voice seem'd calling in her ear,
The night was warm as her desire,
And forth she fled on feet of fire.

One guide ; she had another too :
A crumpled paper coarse to view,
Wherein she had kept with tender care
A little lock of precious hair,

And on the paper this was written plain :

" EUREKA HART, DROWSIETOWN, STATE OF
   MAINE."

O poor dark bird, nought still knew she
Of this wild world's geography !
Less than the swallow sailing home,
Less than the petrel 'mid the foam,
Less than the mallard winging fast
O'er solitary fens and vast,
To seek his birth-place far away
In regions of the midnight day.
She only knew that somewhere *there*,
   In some strange land afar or near,
Under that star serene and fair,
   He waited ; and her soul could hear
His summons ; even as a dove
   Her soul's wild pinions she unfurl'd,
And sought in constancy and love
   Her only refuge in the world !

A footprint—trace it on !—

　　　　　　For days

Her path was on great pasture ways :

League after league of verdurous bloom

Of star-like flowers and faint perfume,

And from her coming leapt in fear

The antelope and dappled deer;

And everywhere around her grew

Ripe fruit and berries that she knew,

While glistening in the golden gleam

Glanced many a mere and running stream.

A happy land of flocks and herds,

And many-colour'd water-birds !

Oft, sailing with her as she went,

The eagle eddied indolent

On soft swift wing ; and with his wild

Dark dewy eye glanced at her child,

Nor till she scream'd and arms upthrew,

Turn'd, and on sullen wing withdrew.

But sweet it was by night to rest
And give her little babe the breast,
And O each night with eyes most dim
She felt one night more near to *him :*
And all the pains of the past day,
With all the perils of the way,
Seem'd as a dream ; and lo ! afar
She saw the smiling of the Star.

'Twere but a weary task to trace
Her footprint on from place to place,
From day to day ; to sing and tell
What daily accidents befell,
What dangers threaten'd her, what eyes
Watch'd her go by in wild surprise,
What prospects blest her, where and when
She look'd on life and met with men.
Enough to say, thro' light and dark,
Straight, as an arrow to its mark,

The woman flew ; wise in the ways
Of her own race, she hid from gaze
When flitting forms against the sky
Warn'd her that Indians might be nigh ;
And when the wild beast dreadful-eyed
Approach'd her, with shrill shriek she cried,
Until the bloody coward shook
Before the red rage of her look.
And tho' the prospect changed all days,
It did not change to *her;* whose gaze
Saw these things only : the white star
On the horizon line afar,
And the quick beckoning of a hand
Out of another, sweeter land.

The long sad road—the way so dreary
The very *Fancy* falters weary !
The very soul is dazed, and shows
Only a gleam of wild tableaux :
In midst of each that shape of woe
Still straggling northward—slow, slow, slow.

. . . A river deep.   She cannot find
A wading-place to suit her mind;
But on the bank sets quietly,
Amid the sunflowers tall as she,
Her little babe: then slips her dress
And stands in mother-nakedness;
Then in a bundle on her head
She ties her raiment yellow and red,
And swimming o'er the waters bright,
With glistening limbs of liquid light,
Sets down her burden dry, and then,
With swift stroke sailing back again,
Seeks the small babe where it doth lie,
And with her right hand holds it high,
While with the other slow she swims,
Trailing her large and liquid limbs;
Then dripping wades to the far shore,
And clothes her loveliness once more . . .

. . . On a lone plain she now is found,
Where troglodytes dwell underground.

Wild settlers peering from their caves,
Like dead men moving in their graves,
Rise round her as she comes, and glare
With hungry eyes thro' horrent hair;
But they are gentle, and they give
Herbs and black bread that she may live,
And in their caves the weary one
Rests till the rising of the sun;
Then the wild shapes around her stand
Reading the paper in her hand,
And point her northward; and she flies
Fleet-footed, while with wandering eyes
They stand and watch her shape fade dim
Across the dark horizon-rim . . .

. . . She stands on a great river's bank,
'Mid noxious weeds and sedges dank;
And on the yellow river's track,
Jagged with teeth like snags jet black,

The ferryman in his great boat,
A speck on the broad waste, doth float,
Approaching to the water's side,
But lengthways drifting with the tide.
She leaps into the boat, and o'er
The waste to the dark further shore,
Slowly they journey; as he rows
The paper to the man she shows,
Who reads; and as she springs to land,
He too points northward with his hand . . .

. . . See, with a crimson glare of light,
A log-town burneth in the night!
And flying forth with all their goods
Into the sandy solitudes,
The people wild, with bloodless cheeks,
Glare at a wanderer who speaks
In a strange tongue; but as they fly
Are dumb, and answer not her cry . . .

. . . Now thro' a land by the red sun
Scorch'd as with fire, the lonely one
Treads slowly; and ere long she hears
The sharp cry of shrill overseers,
Driving black gangs that toiling tramp
Thro' cotton fields and sugar swamp.
Here first the hand of man is raised
To harm her—for with eyes amazed
She nears a City, and is cast
Into a slave-pen foul and vast,
Seized as an Ethiop slave.   From thence
She in an agony intense
Is thrust; but not ere eager eyes
Have mark'd her beauty as a prize.
But God is good, and one blest day
She hears upon the burning way
An aged half-caste burnt and black
Speak in her tongue and answer back.
These twain wring hands upon the road,
And in the stranger's poor abode

She sleeps that night; but with the sun
She wakens, and is pointed on . . .

. . . Now in a waggon great she lies,
And shaded from the brazen skies,
Slowly she jogs, and all at rest
She gives her little babe the breast.
Happy she rests; hears in her dream
The driver's song, the jingling team.
With jet black cheek and bright red lip,
The negro drives and cracks his whip,
Singing plantation hymns to God,
And grinning greetings with a nod . . .

. . . Now, toiling on a dusty way,
She begs her bread from day to day,
And some are good to her and mild,
And most are soften'd by the child.
Once, as she halts at a great door,
Hungry and weary, sick and sore,

A lovely lady white as milk
Glides past her in her rustling silk;
Then pauses, questioning, and sees
The sleeping babe upon her knees,
And takes the paper from her hand,
And reading it doth understand;
Then stoops to *kiss* the child with cold
Kind lips, and gives the mother gold . . .

. . . Now in a mighty boat, among
A crowd of people strange of tongue,
She saileth slow, with wandering sight,
On a vast river day and night;
All day the prospect drifteth past—
Swamp, wood, and meadow, fading fast,—
With lonely huts, and shapes that stand
On the stream's bank, and wave the hand;
All night with eyes that look aloft,
Or close in sleep, she sails; but oft

The blackness takes a deeper frown,
And the wild eyeballs of a town
Flash open as the boat goes by,
And she awakens with a cry . . .

On, on, and on—O the blind quest,
The throbbing heart, the aching breast!
And O the faith, more steadfast far
Than aught on earth, or any star ;
The faith that never ceased to shine,
The strength of constancy divine,
The will that warm'd her as she went
Across a mighty continent,
Unknown, scarce help'd, from land to land,
With that poor paper in her hand !

The vision falls.   The figure fades
Amid the lonely forest glades,
Fringing the mighty inland seas.
I see her still ; and still she flees

Onward, still onward ; tho' the wind
Blows cold, and nature looks unkind :
The dead leaves fall and rot ; the chill
Damp earth-breath clings to vale and hill,
The birds are sailing south ; and hark !
As she fares onward thro' the dark,
The honking wild geese swiftly sail
Amid a slowly gathering gale.
All darkens ; and around her flow
The cold and silence of the Snow.

There, she is lost ; in that white gleam
She fadeth, let her fade, in dream !
Poor bird of the bright summer, now
She feels the kisses on her brow
Of Frost and Fog ; and at her back
Another Shadow keeps the track.
'Tis winter now ; and birds have flown
Southward, to seek a gladder zone ;

One, only one, doth northward fare,
And dreams to find her summer *there*.
God help her! look not! let her go
Into the realm of the Great Snow!

IV

THE JOURNEY'S END.

BACK in a swoon, with haggard face,
Falleth the woman of wild race,
Dumb, cold as stone, her weary eyes
Fix'd as in very death she lies—
While little Phœbe trembling stands,
Wetting her lips, chafing her hands,
Trembling, almost afraid to stir
For wonder, as she looks at her :
So weird, so wild a shape, she seems
Like some sad spirit seen in dreams ;
Beauteous of face beyond belief,
And yet so worn with want and grief.

The clock ticks low within.   Without
The wind still wanders with shrill shout.

The cuckoo strikes the hour—*midnight !*
And Phœbe starteth in affright.

" O what can keep Eureka still ? "
She thinks, and listens with a thrill
For his foot's sound. It doth not come.
The clock ticks low.   All else is dumb.
And still the woman lieth there,
Down drooping in the great arm-chair,
With hanging hands, chin on her breast,
And 'neath her cloak the babe at rest.
She doth not breathe, she doth not moan,
But lieth like a thing of stone.
" O God," thinks Phœbe, deadly white,
" If she be dead ! " and faint with fright,
Chafeth the fingers marble cold
That seem to stiffen in her hold.
She cannot stir, she cannot move,
To wake the maids who sleep above;

Her heart is fluttering in its fear,
" Eureka!   O that he were here!"

[*He* hurries not! Perchance some sense
Of danger may detain him hence.
He would not hasten, if he knew
The curious sight he has to view.
Few mortal husbands, red or white,
Would care to wear his shoes this night.]

" What can she be?" thinks little Phœbe,
" Some Indian tramp—a beggar maybe—
And yet she's got a different mien
To such of these as I have seen.
Her face is like a babe's—she's young,
And she can speak no other tongue
Than Indian.   When she spoke her words
Came like the gurgling notes of birds.
Poor thing! and out on such a night,
When all the world is wild and white

With the Great Snow.   And O, to see
The little babe upon her knee!
I wonder now, if I should take it
From her cold bosom, I should wake it—
Poor little child!"   And as she spake
Those words she saw the baby wake,
Sweet-smiling in the fire's red streaks,
With beaded eyes and rosy cheeks.
Then Phœbe started.   "Why," thought she,
"The babe is near as fair as me!
With just one dark flash on its face
To show the taint of Indian race.
That's strange! Poor little outcast mite!
I guess his *father's* skin is white."
Then, for a moment, Phœbe's mien
Wore an expression icy-keen,
As now in scrutiny amazed
The sleeping woman's hand she raised,
And dropt it quickly, murmuring—
"She is no wife! she wears no ring!"

So for a space her features took
Pure matronhood's Medusa-look,—
That look, so pitiless and lawful,
Which oft makes little women awful;
And which weak women, when they fall,
Dread in their sisters worst of all!
But bless thee, Phœbe, soon the child
Soften'd thy face and made it mild;
To see it lie so bright and pretty,
Thy woman's eyes were moist for pity,
And soon thy tears began to flow—
"Poor soul! and out in the Great Snow!"

E'en as she spake the stranger stirr'd.

The cold lips trembled with no word.
The fingers quiver'd, the great eyes
Open'd in stupefied surprise,
A deep sigh tore her lips apart,
And with a thickly-throbbing heart

She gazed around.   The ruddy light,
The cosy kitchen warm and bright,
The clock's great shining face, the human
Soft kindly eyes of the white woman,
Came like a dream—her eyes she closed
A moment with a moan, and dozed.
Then suddenly her soul was 'ware
Of the wild quest that brought her there!
She open'd eyes—a flush of red
Flash'd to her cheeks so chill and dead—
She murmur'd quick with quivering lips,
And, trembling to the finger tips,
Thrust her chill hand into her breast,
Under the ragged cloak, in quest
Of something precious hidden there!—
'Tis safe,—she draws it forth with care;
A wretched paper, torn and wet,
   Thumb-mark'd with touch of many a hand
'Tis there—'tis safe—she has it yet,
Her heart's sole guide, the amulet,
   That led her lone feet thro' the land!

But first, unto her lips of ice
She holds it eagerly, and thrice
She *kisses* it ; then, with wild eyes
And unintelligible cries,
Holds it to Phœbe.   " Read ! " cries she,
In her own tongue, distractedly ;
And little Phœbe understands,
And takes the paper in her hands,
And on the hearth she stoopeth low,
To read it in the firelight glow.

Now courage, Phœbe ! steel thy spirit !
A blow is coming—thou must bear it !

Slowly, so vilely it is writ,
Her unskill'd eyes decipher it ;
So worn it is with snow and rain,
That scarce a letter now is plain,
And every red and ragged mark
Is smudged with handling, dim, and dark.

" E-U-R-E "—in letters blurr'd
She spells. " *Eureka !* " that's the word.
But why does little Phœbe start
As she reads on ? " *Eureka Hart* "—
His name, her husband's name ; and now
The red blood flames on cheek and brow !
She stops—she quivers—glares wild-eyed
At the red woman at her side,
Who watches *her* with one sick gaze
Of wild entreaty and amaze :
Then she spells on—her features turn
To marble, though her bright eyes burn,
For all the bitter truth grows plain.

" Eureka Hart, Drowsietown, State of
Maine."

First lightning flash of fierce surprise !
It burns her cheek, and blinds her eyes.
Again she looks on the strange creature's
Tall, ragged form and beauteous features.

Next lightning flash, and muffled thunder—
"The baby's skin is white—no wonder!"
And she perceives, as plain as may be,
All the event—down to the baby!
Last flash, the whole dark mystery lighting,—
"Why, it's Eureka's own handwriting!"

Ay, little wife!—and these dim stains
Are life-blood from Eureka's veins;
In blood the words were writ by him,
And see! how faded and how dim!

The woman took her hand. She shook
The touch away with tiger-look,
And trembling gazed upon her. So
She stagger'd underneath the blow,
Watch'd by the stranger's luminous eyes
In mingled stupor and surprise;
Ah! little did the stranger guess
The situation's bitterness,

But in her own wild tongue did say,
" Where is my love ? show me the way ! "

A hand upon the latch.   Both start,—
  The door swings wide—the drift sweeps in.
Footsteps : and lo ! Eureka Hart,
  Snow-cover'd, muffled to the chin.

V.

FACE TO FACE.

WARMLY muffled to the chin there,
   Blind with snow-drift, stamping, waiting,
Dazzled by the light within there,
   Stood the giant oscillating.
Then he closed the door, and turning
   His great back against it, smiled!
Slightly tipsy, not discerning
   The red woman and her child.
By the great eyes dimly blinking,
   Feebly leering at his mate,
Phœbe saw he had been drinking,
   While he hiccup'd, "Guess I'm late!"
So he stood; when, wildly ringing,
   Rose a scream upon the air,

'Twas the Indian woman, springing,
  Gasping, gazing, from her chair.

Round her face the black hair raining,
To her heart the baby straining,
Gasping, gazing, half believing
'Twas some phantom soul-deceiving,
Bound as by a spell she linger'd,
Pointing at him fiery-finger'd ;
And the giant mighty-jointed,
Groan'd and stagger'd as she pointed,
Thinking, while his heart beat quicker,
'Twas some phantom born of liquor ! . . .
While he rubb'd his eyes and mutter'd,
  While he roll'd his eyes distress'd,
O'er the floor a thin form flutter'd,
  Cried, and sank upon his breast!

Phœbe screams. Stagger'd and blinded,
Stands the creature beaver-minded,

While upon his heart reposes
Cheeks he knows full well—Red Rose's !
Half repulsing and half holding,
While her arms are round him folding,
Gaunt he stands in pain afflicted,
An impostor self-convicted !
While her great eyes, upward-looking,
Not reproaching, not rebuking,
Trusting, loving, lustre-pouring,
Happy now, and still adoring,
Burn on his ; and her dark passion
Masters her in the old fashion,
Thrills the frail thin figure, burning
With a lightning flash of yearning,
Lights the worn cheeks and the faded
Forehead with her dark locks shaded,
Thrills, transfigures, seems to lend her
All the soul of her old splendour ;—
So that all the rags upon her,
All the anguish and dishonour,

All the weary days of wandering,
All the weeping, plaining, pondering,
All the sorrow, all the striving
Ne'er a man could face surviving,
All the Past, burns iridescent
In one Rainbow of the Present.
See! she feasts on every feature
Madly, like a famish'd creature,
Reads each line in rapture, reeling
With the frantic bliss of feeling ;
Kindling now her arms are round him,
Murmuring madly, she hath found him,
He is folded close unto her,
And the bliss of God thrills thro' her !

Her white Chief, whom God had brought her
From the shining Big Sea Water,
Her great Chief of the pale races,
With wise tongues and paintless faces !

More than mortal in her seeing,
Glorious, grand, a god-like being!
Nor, tho' Phœbe stands there, looking
Most distractedly rebuking,
Doth this child of the red nation
Comprehend the situation!
Not a thought hath she to move her,
Save that all the quest is over!
He is living, he is near her,
Grander, greater, braver, dearer!
No reproach in her fixed gaze is
While her eyes to his she raises—
Only hungering and thirsting
Of a heart with pleasure bursting;
Only a supreme sensation
Of ecstatic admiration,
Melting in one soul-flush splendid
Years of heart-ache past and ended.

Her white Warrior, her fair Master!
Hers, all hers, despite disaster!

Hers, her own, that she may cry for,
Cling to, smile to, trust in, die for!
Is she *blind?* Hath the glad wonder
Struck her to the soul and stunn'd her?
Sees she not on every feature
The sick horror of the creature?
Sober now, and looking ghastly,
Trembling while his breath comes fastly,
With the cold sweat on his forehead,
Shrinking as from something horrid,
Paralyzed with guilt, despairing,
Not at *her* but Phœbe glaring,
Speechless, helpless, and aghast,
Stands the giant, pinion'd fast.

Yes, her eyes are blindly gleaming
Thro' the warm tears wildly streaming—
Yes, her soul *is* blind (God guide her!);
Hunger, thirst, and grief, have tried her,
She is feeble, not perceiving
Cause for bitterness or grieving;

She is foolish, never guessing
That her visit is distressing,
She is mad, mad, mad, presuming
He has waited for her coming!

No, she will *not* see the horror
Fate hath been preparing for her—
All the little strength remaining
She will wildly spend in straining,
In a rapturous confusion,
To her breast the old delusion.
Hark! her lips speak, words are springing
Like the notes of a bird singing,
Like a fountain sunward throbbing
With a silvern song of sobbing;
Not a word is clear, but all
Rise in rapture, blend, and fall!

Suddenly the rapture falters,
Her hands loosen, her face alters,

Drawing from him softly, quickly,
While he staggers white and sickly,
She, with grace beyond all beauty,
  Doth her ragged cloak unloose,
Then, with looks of loving duty,
  Shows Eureka—the papoose!

Tiny, pink-cheek'd, blushing brightly,
Like a mummy roll'd up tightly;
Puffing cheeks, and fat hands spreaning
In an ecstasy unmeaning;
Blinking, his pink cheeks in gathers,
With *blue* eyes just like his father's!
In his pretty face already
Just the image of his daddy!
Stolid, stretching hands to pat him,
Lies the baby, smiling at him!

Still stands little Phœbe, panting,
This, and only this, was wanting;

Now, with all her courage rallied,
She between them—panting, pallid—
Stands ; and, keen-eyed as an eagle,
　Tho' as fluttering as a linnet,
Folds her virtue, like a regal
　Robe, around her ; frowning in it.
Yet so wildly doth she flutter,
Not a sentence can she utter ;
Stately, speechless, with eyes blazing,
Stands the little White Rose, gazing !

Suddenly, with acclamation,
On that group of desperation
Bursts the Storm !—With one wild rattle
Of the elements at battle,
With one horrid roar and yelling,
Tearing, tugging at the dwelling,
Strikes the Wind ; the latch is lifted,
　With a crash wide swings the door ;
In the blinding Snow is drifted,
　With a melancholy roar !

'Tis the elements of Nature
Flocking round the weary creature,
Crying to her, while they blind her,
"Come to *us !* for we are kinder!
Cross the cruel, fatal portal
Of the miserable mortal;
Come, our hands are cold but loving!
Back into the midnight moving,
In some spot of silence creeping,
Find a quiet place for sleeping.
We, the Winds, will dig it straightway,
Far beyond the white man's gateway.
I, the Snow, will place above it
My soft cheek, and never move it;
With my beauty, white and chilly,
Lying o'er thee like a lily,
Dress'd for sleep in snowy clothing
Thou shalt slumber, hearing nothing.
We will freeze thine ears from hearing
His hard foot when it is nearing;

We will close thine eyes from conning
His that look upon thee shunning.
We will keep thee, we will guard thee,
Till the kiss of God reward thee.
Come, O come!" Thus, unavailing,
Sounds the elemental wailing.

Peace, O Winds, your weary voices
Teach her nothing : she rejoices!
Hush, O Snow, let your chill hands not
Touch her cheek ; she understands not!
Hush!   But God, who is that other,
    Standing beckoning unto her?
Winds and Snows, 'tis your pale brother,
    And his chilly breath thrills thro' her.
Ay, the Shadow there is looming
Thro' the tempest and the glooming!
O'er each path her feet have chosen—
Mountains, valleys, rivers frozen ;

Creeping near, with eyes that glisten,
When her cold foot flagg'd, to listen;
As a bloodhound, ever flitting,
Night-time, day-time, never quitting;
Sure of scent, with thin foot trailing
In the snowdrift, never failing,
He has follow'd, follow'd slow,
That red footprint in the Snow!
Now he finds her white and wan,—
'Tis the Winter, Peboan.

Spare her! Who would bid him spare her?
Let him trance her and upbear her
In his arms, and softly place her
Where no cruel foot may trace her.
Let her die! See, his eyes con her,
And his icy hand is on her;
Thro' her form runs the quick shiver,
Light as leaves her eyelids quiver,

And with quick, spasmodic touches,
The belovèd form she clutches;
From the cruelty of man,
Take her gently, Peboan!

Phœbe shivers. To her reaching,
With an agony beseeching,
Red Rose holds the babe; one moment,
With a shrug of bitter comment,
Phœbe shrinks; then, being human,
  Frighten'd, thinking Death is there,
Quietly the little woman
  Takes the burden unaware.
Not a breath too soon; for, rocking
  In the roaring of the storm,
With the snow flakes round her flocking,
  And the wild wind round her form,
With a cry of anguish, prone
Falls the wanderer, cold as stone!

VI.

PAUGUK.

O poor Red Rose! rent by the storm!
The flame still flickered in her form.

Moveless she lay; but in her breast
The tumult was not quite at rest.

They raised her up, and, with soft tread,
They bore her slowly to a bed.

And little Phœbe's heart did ache,
Despite her wrongs, for pity's sake;

And little Phœbe's own kind hands
(God bless them!) loosed the wand'rer's bands,

Took softly off the dripping dress,
With eyes that wept for kindliness,

Wrung the wet hair, and smoothed it right,
And clad the Red Rose all in white.

There, all in white, on a white bed,
The Red Rose hung her heavy head.

Around her was a roar, a gleam,
And she was struggling in a dream.

Faces round her went and came,
Her great eyes flash'd with fading flame.

For all the time, fever'd and sore,
She did her journey yet once more;

Once again her Soul's feet trod
The pathless wild, the weary road;

Once again she sail'd along
The mighty meres and rivers strong;

Once again, with weary tread,
She stagger'd on, and begged her bread;

Once again she falter'd slow
Into the realm of the Great Snow.

Oh, the roaring in her brain!
Oh, the wild winds that moan again!

Against her, as she clasps her child,
The hail is driven, the drift is piled.

She sees a light that shines afar;
It beckons her—a hand, a Star.

She hears a voice afar away;
It calls to her; she must not stay.

Around her clouds of tempest roll,
And, oh ! the storm within her soul !

But now and then, amid the snow,
There comes a silence and a glow ;

And white she lies, in a white room,
And some one watches in the gloom.

Close by the bed where she doth rest,
Sits, with the babe upon her breast,

A little woman, waiting there,
Despite her wrongs, so kind, so fair !

E'en as she wakens, wild and weak,
Red Rose sits up, and tries to speak,

And reaching out, with a thin moan,
She takes a white hand in her own ;

But swoons once more, and hears again
The tempest roaring in her brain!

Now as she dreams, with fever'd cries,
Phœbe looks on with quiet eyes;

And Phœbe and her maidens go
Softly and lightly to and fro.

Down-stairs by the great fire of wood,
Alone, Eureka Hart doth brood;

And when his little wife descends
He scowls, and eyes his finger-ends.

She scarcely looks into his face,
But orders him about the place;

And at her will he flies full meek,
With red confusion on his cheek.

Her eyes are swoll'n with tears ; to him
Her face is pitiless and grim.

But as she reascends the stairs
Her pale cheek flushes unawares.

In pity half, and half in scorn,
She sees again that shape forlorn.

She cannot love her ; yet her heart
Flutters, and takes the wand'rer's part.

Her thoughts are angry, weak and wild,
Yet carefully she tends the child.

Often she prays, with heart astir,
The white man's God to strengthen her.

And thus, despite her heart's distress,
She doth a deed of blessedness.

Silent for days by that bedside
She waiteth, watching, weary-eyed :

Not all alone ; by her unseen,
Sitteth another, strange of mien.

He squatteth in the corner there,
And looketh on through his thin hair.

Clad in fantastic Indian weeds,
With calumet and skirt of beads,

Gaunt, haggard, hungry, woebegone,
Waiteth Pauguk, the Skeleton !

For wintry Peboan hath fled,
Leaving this shadow in his stead.

And there he waits, unseen, unheard ;
And as a serpent on a bird

Fixeth his glittering gaze, Pauguk
Watcheth the bed with hungry look.

VII.

THE MELTING OF THE SNOW

A SOUND of streamlets flowing, flowing ;
A cry of winds so bleakly blowing ;
A stir, a tumult ever growing ;
Deep night ; and the Great Snow was going.

Underneath her death-shroud thick,
Like a body buried quick,
Heaved the Earth, and thrusting hands
Crack'd the ice and brake her bands.
Heaven, with face of watery woe,
Watched the resurrection grow.
All the night, bent to be free,
In a sickening agony,

Struggled Earth.   With silent tread
From his cold seat at her head
Rose the Frost, and northward stole
To his cavern near the pole.
When the bloodshot eyes of Morn
Opened in the east forlorn,
'Twas a dreary sight to see
Blotted waste and watery lea,
All the beautiful white plains
Blurr'd with black'ning seams and stains,
All the sides of every hill
Scarr'd with thaw and dripping chill,
All the cold sky scowling black
O'er the soaking country track;
There a sobbing everywhere
In the miserable air,
And a thick fog brooding low
O'er the black trail of the snow;
While the Earth, amid the gloom
Still half buried in her tomb,

Swooning lay, and could not rise,
With dark film upon her eyes.

In the farmhouse (where a light
Glimmer'd feebly day and night
From the sick-room) Red Rose heard
Earth's awakening, and stirr'd,
Gazed around her, and descried
Phœbe sitting at her side,
Knitting, while the little child,
Sleeping on the pillow, smiled.
Little Phœbe's face was still,
Calm with quiet strength and will.
And the lamplight round her flitted
Faintly, feebly, as she knitted.
Full confession had she brought
From Eureka's soul distraught.
What he hid, in desperation,
She supplied, by penetration.

So she traced from the beginning
All the story of the sinning.
Had her spirit felt perchance
Just a little more romance ;
Had the giant in her sight
Seem'd a paragon more bright ;
Had the married love she bore
Been a very little more—
Why, perchance poor Phœbe's heart
Might have taken the man's part,
Heaping fiercely, as is common,
All its hate upon the woman.
Not so Phœbe! cold and pale
Did she listen to the tale ;
Ne'er relenting, scarcely heeding,
Heard the man's excusing, pleading ;
Felt her blood boil, and her face
Crimson for a moment's space,
Thinking darkly, in dismay,
" What will Parson Pendon say ? "

But at last the little soul
Back to the sick chamber stole ;
Saw the wanderer lying there,
Wildly, marvellously fair ;
Saw the little baby too
Blinking with big eyes of blue ;
And she murmured, with a sigh,
" She's deceived, as well as I.
Hers is far the bitterest blow,
'Cause she seems to love him so."
So thought Phœbe, calmly sitting
By the bedside at her knitting,
While the fog hung thick and low
O'er the black trail of the Snow.

Thus she did her duty there,
Tending with a bitter care
Her sick rival ; spite her pain,
Able, with a woman's brain,
To discern as clear as day

On whose side the sinning lay ;
Able to compassionate
Her deluded rival's fate,
All the weariness and care
Of the fatal journey there ;
Able to acknowledge (this
Far the most amazing is)
On how dull and mean a thing
Wasted was this passioning ;
On how commonplace a chance
Hung the wanderer's romance ;
Round how mere a Log did twine
The wild tendrils of this vine.

Screen'd thus from the wintry blast,
Droopt the Red Rose, fading fast ;
While the White Rose, hanging near,
Trembled in a pensive fear.
So the snow had nearly fled,
And upon her dying bed

Earth was quick'ning; damp and chill
Streamed the fog on vale and hill.
Like a slimy crocodile
Weltering on banks o' Nile,
Everywhere, with muddy maw,
Crawl'd the miserable Thaw.
On the pond and on the stream
Loosen'd lights began to gleam,
And before the snow could fleet
Drizzly rains began to beat.

Here and there upon the plain,
'Mid the pools of thaw and rain,
Linger'd in the dismal light
Patches of unmelted white.
As these melted, very slowly,
In a quiet melancholy,
Vacant gleams o' the clouded blue
Through the dismal daylight flew,
And the wind, with a shrill clang,
Went into the west, and sang.

A sound of waters ever flowing;
A stir, a tumult, ever growing;
A gleam o' the blue, a west wind blowing;
Warmth, and the last snow wreath was going.

Not alone! ah! not alone!

Waking up with fever'd moan,
Red Rose started and looked round,
Listening for a voice, a sound,
And the skeleton, Pauguk,
Crouching silent in his nook,
Panted, like a famish'd thing,
In the very act to spring.

'Twas at sunset; on the bed
Crimson shafts of light were shed,
And the face, famish'd and thin,
Flash'd to sickly flame therein,
While the eyes, with fevered glare,
Sought a face they saw not there.

Then she moan'd, and with a cry,
Beckoning little Phœbe nigh,
Whisper'd ; but the words she said
Perish'd uninterpreted.
Still, in bitterest distress,
Clinging to poor Phœbe's dress,
With wild gestures, she in vain
Tried to make her meaning plain.
Then did little Phœbe see
How the face changed suddenly!
For invisible Pauguk,
Creeping swiftly from his nook,
Stood erect, and hung the head
O'er the woman on the bed.
Still the woman, glaring round,
Listen'd for a voice, a sound,
Crying wildly o'er and o'er,
With her great eyes on the door.

Pale, affrighted, and aghast,
Phœbe understood at last—

Knew the weary wanderer cried
To behold *him* ere she died ;
So, without a word of blame,
Phœbe called him, and he came.

The sun was set, the night was growing,
Softly the wind o' the west was blowing,
The gates of heaven were overflowing ;
With the last snow Red Rose was going.

VIII

THE LAST LOOK.

To the bedside, white and quaking,
   Came Eureka, with a groan,
Conscience-stricken now, and taking
   Her thin hand into his own.
At the touch she kindled, rallied,
   With a look of gentle grace ;
Clung about him deathly pallid,
   And, uplooking in his face,
Smiled !   Ah, God ! that smile of parting
From her soul's dim depths upstarting !
'Twas a smile of awful beauty,
Full of fatal love and duty ;

Such a smile as haunts for ever
Any being but a beaver.
Ev'n Eureka's stolid spirit
Was half agonized to bear it.
Smiling thus, and softly crooning
   Words he could not understand,
Sank she on the pillow, swooning,
   Clutching still her hero's hand.

Silent Spirits, shapes that love her,
Is she resting? is all over?
Nay; for while Eureka, quaking,   .
   Heart-sick, soul-sick to behold her,
From the bed her worn form taking,
   Leans her head upon his shoulder;
Once again, the spirit flying,
   With a last expiring ray,
Waves a message, dimly dying,
   From its tenement of clay.
Those great eyes upon him looking,
Not reproaching, not rebuking,

Brighten into bliss—perceiving
Nought of shame or of deceiving :
Only for the last time seeing
Her great Chief, a god-like being ;
Only happy, all at rest,
To be dying—on his breast.

See ! her hand points upward, slowly,
With an awful grace and holy,
And her eyes are saying clearly,
" Master, lord, beloved so dearly,
We shall meet, with souls grown fonder,
In God's happy prairies yonder ;
Where no Snow falls ; where, for ever,
Flows the shining Milky River,
On whose banks, divinely glowing,
Shapes like ours are coming, going,
In the happy star-dew moving,
Silent, smiling, loved, and loving !
Fare thee well, till then, my Master ! "

Hark, her breath comes fainter, faster,

While, in love man cannot measure,

   Kissing her white warrior's hand,

She sinks, with one great smile of pleasure—

   Last flash upon the blackening brand!

Epilogue.

EPILOGUE.

In a dark corner of the burial-place,
Where sleep apart the creatures of red race,
Red Rose was laid, cold, beautiful, and dead,
With all the great white Snow above her bed.
And soon the tiny partner of her quest,
The little babe, was laid upon her breast;
For, though the heart of Phœbe had been kind,
And sought to save the infant left behind,
It wither'd when the mother's kiss withdrew—
The Red Rose faded, and the Blossom too.
There sleeps their dust, but 'neath another sky,
More kind than this, their Spirits sleeping lie.

Sleeping, or waking? *There*, with eyes tear-wet,
Is her soul homeless? doth she wander yet,

Silent by those still pathways, with bent head,
Still listening, listening, for her warrior's tread?
It came not, comes not—tho' the ages roll,
Still with that life-long hunger in her soul,
She must wait on, and thousand others too,
If waking Immortality be true.
But, no; God giveth his belovèd sleep;
Rose of the wilderness, may thine be deep!
Not near the white man's happy Death-domains,
But in the red man's mighty hunting-plains;
Amid the harmless shades of flocks and herds,
Amid the hum of bees, the song of birds,
With fields and woods all round, and skies above
Dark as thine eyes, and deathless as thy love!

Here ends my tale; what further should I state?
Save that poor Phœbe soon forgave her mate,
As small white wives forgive; with words out-
    spoken
The peace was patch'd almost as soon as broken;

For Phœbe argued, after a good cry,
" 'Tis a bad job ; but break my heart—not I !
All the men do it—that's a fact confess'd,
And my great stupid's only like the rest.
But what's the good of fretting more than need ?
I've got the cows to mind, the hens to feed.
I 'spose it's dreadful, but 'tis less a sin
Than if the wench had a white woman's skin ! "
Oft at his head her mocking shafts she aim'd,
While by the hearth he hung the head ashamed,
Pricking his moral hide right thro' and thro',
As virtuous little wives so well can do,
Till out he swagger'd, cursing, sorely hit,
And puzzled by the little woman's wit.
Indeed, for seasons of domestic strife,
She kept this rod in pickle all her life.

As for Eureka, why, he felt, of course,
Some conscience-prick, some tremor of remorse,
Not deep enough to cause him many groans,

R

Or keep the fat from growing on his bones.

He throve, he prosper'd, was esteem'd by all,—

At fifty, he was broad as he was tall ;

Loved much his pipe and glass, and at the inn

Spake oft—an oracle of double chin.

Did he forget her ? Never ! Often, while

He sat and puff'd his pipe with easy smile,

Surveying fields and orchards from the porch,

And far away the little village church,

While all seem'd peaceful—earth, and air, and
    sky,—

A twinkle came into his fish-like eye;

" Poor critter ! " sigh'd he, as a cloud he blew,

" She was a splendid figure, and that's true ! "

NOTES.

P. 209.

" Puffing cheeks and fat hands *spreaning*."

The Printer's Devil queries this, but he does not know the Old Poets. See (*e.g.*) Michael Drayton's " Moses' Birth and Miracles" —" And *spreans* the pretty hands."

P. 213.

" 'Tis the Winter, Peboan."

See the American-Indian Mythology. " Peboan " is the personification of extreme Cold.

P. 215.

" Pauguk, the Skeleton."

In the same mythology, Pauguk is, as represented in the poem, the Indian spirit of DEATH.

VIRTUE AND CO., PRINTERS, CITY ROAD, LONDON.

Now Ready, the Fourth Edition of

SAINT ABE:

𝔄 𝔗𝔞𝔩𝔢 𝔬𝔣 𝔖𝔞𝔩𝔱 𝔏𝔞𝔨𝔢 ℭ𝔦𝔱𝔶.

TESTIMONIES OF DISTINGUISHED PERSONS.

I. FROM P———T G——T, U.S.

Smart. Polygamy is Greek for Secesh. Guess Brigham will have to make tracks.

II. FROM R. W. E——N, BOSTON, U.S.

Adequate expression is rare. I had fancied the oracles were dumb, and had returned with a sigh to the enervating society of my friends in Boston, when your book reached me. To think of it! In this very epoch, at this very day, poetry has been secreting itself silently and surely, and suddenly the whole ocean of human thought is illumined by the accumulated phosphorescence of a subtle and startling poetic life. . . . Your work is the story of Polygamy written in colossal cipher for the study of all forthcoming ages. Triflers will call you a caricaturist, empty solemnities will deem you a jester. Fools! who miss the pathetic symbolism of Falstaff, and deem the Rabelaisan epos fit food for mirth. . . . I read it from first page to last with solemn thoughts too deep for tears. I class you already with the creators, with Shakespere, Dante, Whitman, Ellery Channing, and myself.

III. FROM W———T W———N, WASHINGTON, U.S.

1 Our own feuillage;
   A leaf from the sweating branches of these States;
   A fallen symbol, I guess, vegetable, living, human;
   A heart-beat from the hairy breast of a man.

2 The Salon contents me not ;
  The fine feathers of New England damsels content me not ;
  The ways of snobs, the falsettos of the primo tenore, the legs
    of Lydia Thomson's troupe of blondes, content me not ;
  Nor tea-drinking, nor the twaddle of Mr. Secretary Harlan,
    nor the loafers of the hotel bar, nor Sham, nor Long-
    fellow's Village Blacksmith.

3 But the Prairies content me ;
  And the Red Indian dragging along his squaw by the scruff of
    the neck ;
  And the bones of mules and adventurous persons in Bitter
    Creek ;
  And the oaths of pioneers, and the ways of the unwashed,
    large, undulating, majestic, virile, strong of scent, all
    these content me.

4 Utah contents me ;
  The City by the margin of the great Salt Lake contents me ;
  And to have many wives contents me ;
  Blessed is he who has a hundred wives, and peoples the
    solitudes of these States.

5 Great is Brigham ;
  Great is polygamy, great is monogamy, great is polyandry,
    great is license, great is right, and great is wrong ;
  And I say again that wrong is every whit as good as right, and
    not one jot better ;
  And I say further there is no such thing as wrong, nor any
    such thing as right, and that neither are accountable, and
    that both exist only by allowance.

6 O I am wonderful ;
  And the world, and the sea, and joy and sorrow, and sense
    and nonsense, all content me ;
  And this book contents me, with its feuillage from the City of
    many wives.

IV. FROM ELDER F——K E——S, OF MT. L———N, U.S.

An amusing attempt to show that polygamy is a social failure.
None can peruse it without perceiving at once that the author
secretly inclines to the ascetic tenets of Shakerism.

V. FROM BROTHER T. H. N———S, O———A C——K.

After perusing this subtle study, who can doubt that Free Love
is the natural human condition ? The utter selfishness of the

wretched monogamist-hero repels and sickens us ; nor can we look with anything but disgust on the obtusity of the heroine, in whom the author vainly tries to awaken interest. It is quite clear that the reconstruction of Utah on O——a C—k principles would yet save the State from the crash which is impending.

VI. From E——a F——nh——m, of S——n Island.

If *Polygamy* is to continue, then, I say, let *Polyandry* flourish ! Woman is the sublimer Being, the subtler Type, the more delicate Mechanism, and strictly speaking *needs* many pendants of the inferior or masculine Type to fulfil her mission in perfect comfort. Shall Brigham Young, a mere Man, have sixteen wives, and shall one wretched piece of humanity content *me*, that supreme Fact, *a perfect Woman*, highest and truest of beings under God ? No ; if these things be tolerated, I claim for each Woman, in the name of Light and Law, twenty ministering attendants of the lower race ; and the day is near when, if this boon, or any other boon we like to ask, be denied us, it will be *taken with a strong hand !*

VII. From T——s C——e, Esq., Chelsea, England.

The titanic humour of the Conception does not blind me to the radical falseness of the Teaching, wherein, as I shall show you presently, you somewhat resemble the miserable Homunculi of our own literary Wagners ; for if I rightly conceive, you would tacitly and by inference urge that it is expressly part of the Divine Thought that the *Ewigweibliche*, or Woman-Soul, should be *happy*. Now Woman's *mundane* unhappiness, as I construe, comes of her Inadequacy ; it is the stirring within her of the Infinite against the Finite, a struggle of the spark upward, of the lower to the higher Symbol. Will Woman's Rights Agitators, and Monogamy, and Political Tomfoolery, do what Millinery has failed to do, and waken one Female to the sense of divine Function ? It is not *happiness* I solicit for the Woman-Soul, but *Identity ;* and the prerogative of Identity is great work, Adequacy, pre-eminent fulfilment of the Function ; woman in this country of rags and shams being buried quick under masses of Sophistication and Upholstery, oblivious of her divine duty to increase the population and train the young masculine Idea starward. I do not care if the wives of Deseret are pale, or faint, or uncultured, or unhappy ; it is enough for me to know that they have a numerous progeny and believe in Deity or the Divine Essence ; and I will not conclude this letter without recording my conviction that yonder man, Brigham Young by name, is perhaps the clearest Intellect now brooding on this planet ; that Freidrich was royaller but not greater, and that Bismarck is no more than his equal ; and that he, this American, few in words, mark you, but great in deeds, has decided a more stupendous

Question than ever puzzled the strength of either of those others,—
the Question of the Sphere and Function in modern life of the ever
agitating FEMININE PRINCIPLE. If furthermore, as I have ever
held, the test of clearness of intellect and greatness of soul be
Success, at any price and under any circumstances, none but a
transcendental Windbag or a pedantic Baccalaureus will doubt my
assertion that Young is a stupendous intellectual, ethical, and
political Force—a Master-Spirit—a Colossal Being, a moral Archi-
tect of sublime cunning—as such to be reverenced by every right-
thinking *Man* under the Sun.

VIII. FROM J——N R——N, ESQ., LONDON.

I am not generally appreciated in my own country, because I
frequently change my views about religion, art, architecture, poetry,
and things in general. Most of my early writings are twaddle,
but my present opinions are all valuable. I think this poem, with
its nervous Saxon Diction, its subtle humour, its tender pathos and
piteousness, the noblest specimen of narrative verse of modern
times ; and indeed I know not where to look, out of the pages of
Chaucer, for an equally successful blending of human laughter and
ethereal mystery. At the same time, the writer scarcely does
justice to the subject on the æsthetic side. A City where the
streets are broad and clean and well-watered, the houses surrounded
by gardens full of fruit and flowers ; where the children, with
shining, clean-washed faces, curtsey to the Philosophers in the
public places ; where there are no brothels and no hells ; where
life runs fresh, free, and unpolluted,—such a City, I say, can hardly
be the symbol of feminine degradation. More than once, tired of
publishing my prophetic warnings in the *Daily Telegraph*, I have
thought of bending my weary footsteps to the new Jerusalem ; and
I might have carried out my intention long ago, if I had had a less
profound sense of my own unfitness for the duties of a Saint.

IX. FROM M——W A——D, ESQ., ENGLAND.

Your poem possesses a certain rough primitive humour, though
it appears to me deficient in the higher graces of *sweetness* and
light. St. Paul would have entirely objected to the monogamical
inference drawn in your epilogue ; and the fact that you draw any
such inference at all is to me a distressing proof that your tendency
is to the Philistinism of those authors who write for the British
Matron. I fear you have not read " Merope."

Fourth Edition, enlarged and revised.   Crown 8vo, 5s.

SAINT ABE:

A Tale of Salt Lake City.

———◆———

OPINIONS OF THE PRESS.

From the "GRAPHIC."

"Such vigorous, racy, determined satire has not been met with
for many a long day.   It is at once fresh and salt as the sea. . . . .
The humour is exquisite, and as regards literary execution, the
work is masterly."

From the "PALL MALL GAZETTE."

"Although in a striking address to Chaucer the author intimates
an expectation that Prudery may turn from his pages, and though
his theme is certainly a delicate one, there is nothing in the book
that a modest man may not read without blinking, and therefore,
we suppose, no modest woman.   On the other hand, the whole
poem is marked with so much natural strength, so much of the
inborn faculties of literature—(though they are wielded in a light,
easy, trifling way)—that they take possession of our admiration as
of right.   The chief characteristics of the book are mastery of
verse, strong and simple diction, delicate, accurate description of
scenery, and that quick and forcible discrimination of character
which belongs to men of dramatic genius.   This has the look of
exaggerated praise.   We propose, therefore, to give one or two
large samples of the author's quality, leaving our readers to judge
from them whether we are not probably right.   If they turn to the
book and read it through, we do not doubt that they will agree
with us."

From the "ILLUSTRATED REVIEW."

"The tale, however, is not to be read from reviews. . . . The
variety of interest, the versatility of fancy, the richness of description with which the different lays and cantos are replete, will
preclude the possibility of tediousness.   To open the book is to
read it to the end.   It is like some Greek comedy in its shifting
scenes, its vivid pictures, its rapidly-passing 'dramatis personæ'
and supernumeraries. . . . The author of 'St. Abe,' who can write
like this, may do more if he will, and even found a new school of
realistic and satirical poetry."

From the " DAILY NEWS."

" If the author of a 'Tale of Salt Lake City ' be not a new poet, he is certainly a writer of exceedingly clever and effective verses. They have the ring of originality, and they indicate ability to produce something still more remarkable than this very remarkable little piece. It merits a place among works which every one reads with genuine satisfaction. It is a piece which subserves one of the chief ends of poetry, that of telling a tale in an unusually forcible and pleasant way. . . . If it be the author's purpose to furnish a new argument against polygamous Mormons, by showing the ridiculous side of their system, he has perfectly succeeded. The extracts we have given show the varied, fluent, and forcible character of his verse. None who read about Saint Abe and his Seven Wives can fail to be amused and to be gratified alike by the manner of the verse and the matter of the tale."

From the " SCOTSMAN."

" This book does not need much commendation, but it deserves a great deal. The author of 'The Biglow Papers ' might have written it, but there are passages which are not unlike Bret Harte ; and him we suspect. The authorship, however, may be left out of notice. Men inquire who has written a good book, that they may honour him ; but if his name be never heard, the book is none the less prized. In design and construction this work has high merit. It is a good story and it is good poetry. The author is a humorist and a satirist, and he has here displayed all his qualities lavishly."

From the " NONCONFORMIST."

" Amazingly clever. . . . Besides, its pure tone deserves warm recognition. The humour is never coarse. There is a high delicacy, which is sufficient to colour and sweeten the whole, as the open spring breeze holds everything in good savour."

From the " SPECTATOR."

" We believe that the new book which has just appeared, ' St. Abe and His Seven Wives,' will paralyze Mormon resistance far more than any amount of speeches in Congress or messages from President Grant, by bringing home to the minds of the millions the ridiculous-diabolic side of the peculiar institution. The canto called ' The Last Epistle of St. Abe to the Polygamists,' with its humorous narrative of the way in which the Saint, sealed to seven wives, fell in love with one, and thenceforward could not abide the jealousy felt by the other six, will do more to weaken the last defence of Mormonism—that after all, the women like it—than a whole ream of narratives about the discontent in Utah. Thousands on whom narrative and argument would make little or no impression, will feel how it must be when many wives with burning hearts watch the husband's love growing for one, when the favourite is sick unto death, and how 'they set their lips and sneered at me and watched the situation,' and will understand that the first price paid for polygamy is the suppression of love, and the second, the slavery of women. The letter in which the first point is proved is too long for quotation, and would be spoiled by extracts ; but the second could hardly be better proved than in these humorous lines. . . . The descriptions of Saint Abe and his Seven Wives will be relished by roughs in California as much as by the self-indulgent philosophers of Boston. . . . Pope would have been proud, we fancy, of these terrible lines, uttered by a driver whose *fiancée* has just been beguiled away by a Mormon saint."

From the "ATHENÆUM."

"'Saint Abe and his Seven Wives' has a freshness and an originality, altogether wanting in Mr. Longfellow's new work, 'The Divine Tragedy.' In quaint and forcible language—language admirably suited to the theme—the author takes us to the wondrous city of the saints, and describes its inhabitants in a series of graphic sketches. The hero of the story is Saint Abe, or Abraham Clewson, and in giving us his history the author has really given us the inner life of the Mormon settlement. In his pages we see the origin of the movement, the reasons why it has increased, the internal weakness of the system, and the effect it produces on its adherents. We are introduced to the saints, whom we see among their pastures, in their homes, in their promenades, and in their synagogue."

From the "FREEMAN."

" A remarkable poem. . . . The production is anonymous, but whoever the author may be there can be no question that he is a poet, and one of vast and varied powers. The inner life of Mormondom is portrayed with a caustic humour equal to anything in ' The Biglow Papers ; ' and were it not for the exquisite elegance of the verse we should think that some parts of the poem were written by Robert Browning. The hero of the poem is a Mormon, who fares so badly as a polygamist that he elopes with one of his seven wives—the one whom he really loves ; and the story is a most effective exposure of the evils which necessarily attach to polygamy."

From the "WEEKLY REVIEW."

" There can be no doubt that it is worthy of the author of ' The Biglow Papers.' Since that work was published, we have received many humorous volumes from across the Atlantic, but nothing equal to ' St. Abe.' As to its form, it shows that Mr. Lowell has been making advances in the poetic art ; and the substance of it is as strong as anything in the entire range of English satirical literature."

From the " BRITISH QUARTERLY REVIEW."

" The writer has an easy mastery over various kinds of metre, and a felicity of easy rhyming which is not unworthy of our best writers of satire. . . . The prevailing impression of the whole is of that easy strength which does what it likes with language and rhythm. . . . . The style is light and playful, with admirable touches of fine discrimination and rich humour ; but the purpose is earnest. . . . . The book is a very clever and a very wholesome one. It is one of those strong, crushing, dramatic satires, which do more execution than a thousand arguments."

From " TEMPLE BAR."

" It is said to be by Lowell. Truly if America has more than one writer who can write in such a rich vein of satire, humour, pathos, and wit, as we have here, England must look to her laurels. . . . This is poetry of a high order. Would that in England we had humorists who could write as well. But with Thackeray our last writer of humour left us."

From the " WESTMINSTER REVIEW."

" ' Saint Abe and his Seven Wives ' may lay claim to many rare qualities. The author possesses simplicity and directness. To this he adds genuine humour and intense dramatic power. Lastly, he has contrived to give a local flavour, something of the salt of the Salt Lake to his characters, which enables us to thoroughly realise them. . . . We will not spoil the admirable canto ' Within the Synagogue ' by any quotation, which however long cannot possibly do it justice. We will merely say that this one bit is worth the price of the whole book. In the author we recognise a true poet with an entirely original vein of humour."

From the " MANCHESTER GUARDIAN."

" It is thoroughly American, now rising into a true imaginative intensity, but oftener falling into a satirical vein, dealing plainly enough with the plague-spots of Salt Lake society and its wily, false prophets. . . . Like most men capable of humour, the author has command of a sweeter and more harmonious manner. Indeed, the beautiful descriptive and lyrical fragments stand in vivid and refreshing relief to the homely staple of the poem."

From the " TORONTO GLOBE."

" It is impossible to deny that the praises bestowed on ' St. Abe and his Seven Wives ' as a work of literary power are deserved."

www.ingramcontent.com/pod-product-compliance
Lightning Source LLC
Chambersburg PA
CBHW020353030726
47496CB00007B/2123